I0740090

the BITE OF WINTER

A LOVE BITES NOVELLA

LAUREN SMITH

DEDICATION

For my parents, Ken and Julie, who spend hours talking about writing and strategizing with me on how to make my dreams come true, even when they have to make sacrifices of their own. Thank you for everything you've given me, including the courage to fight for my dreams. For Jeanne and Angela who are two wonderful beta readers. You ladies rock!

OTHER TITLES BY LAUREN SMITH

HISTORICAL

The League of Rogues Series
Wicked Designs
His Wicked Seduction
Her Wicked Proposal
Wicked Rivals
His Wicked Secret (coming soon)
The Seduction Series
The Duelist's Seduction
The Rakehell's Seduction
The Rogue's Seduction (coming soon)
Standalone Stories
Tempted by A Rogue

CONTEMPORARY

The Surrender Series
The Gilded Cuff
The Gilded Cage
The Gilded Chain
Her British Stepbrother
Forbidden: Her British Stepbrother
Seduction: Her British Stepbrother
Climax: Her British Stepbrother

PARANORMAL

Dark Seductions Series
The Shadows of Stormclyffe Hall
The Love Bites Series
The Bite of Winter
Brotherhood of the Blood Moon Series
Blood Moon on the Rise

SCI-FI ROMANCE

Cyborg Genesis Series
Across the Stars (coming 2017)

CHAPTER ONE

SO HUNGRY. GOD, I'D KILL to eat.

Zoey Blake gazed longingly through the diner window. Families were nestled in red leather booths, plates of burgers and fries spread out like a feast. The light from the diner beckoned to her, promising warmth and comfort. It was everything she wanted, and everything she couldn't have.

The harsh December wind cut through her thin flannel shirt and whipped her hair hard enough to sting her face. Hunger swelled up inside her like an empty balloon. A moan escaped her lips as she tried and failed to ignore the pain.

A little boy in one of the booths reached with chubby hands to grab his mother's milkshake. He sucked for a long moment on the straw before pulling back, a grin of delight on his face. Zoey could imagine the thick creamy ice cream and the sweet tangy taste of a maraschino cherry.

One of the cooks left the grill and walked toward the entrance, wiping his hands on his greasy apron. When the door swung open, Christmas music exploded into the street. The happy sounds reminded Zoey that Christmas was only a few weeks away. She used to love Christmas: the songs, the presents, the food…her family. She shuddered and buried the painful memories deep inside her.

The cook glanced down the empty street outside the diner and caught sight of her.

"You coming in?" His gruff voice momentarily distracted her

from the greasy smell of food.

Zoey gulped and took an instinctive step back, her hands clutching the only real possession she had left in the world. A black leather portfolio. She'd tucked it safely against her chest, the leather barely holding warmth to her body.

"Sorry, I…I can't…" She couldn't say the words. *Can't afford it.*

Even after a year of living on the streets, shame still heated her cheeks. This time, she welcomed it. She was cold all the time, even in the summer. Her jacket had been stolen the winter before, leaving her painfully exposed.

The cook's eyes hardened.

"Then get going. You're scaring off paying customers."

Of course she had to leave. Heaven forbid he toss her some of the burnt burgers or even some moldy buns. She'd have gladly taken them. Far worse food had ended up in her stomach when she'd been desperate.

With a shaky nod, Zoey backed away from the diner and eased into the shadows where the restaurant's light couldn't penetrate. She just wanted to disappear. No one would miss her. No one would care. Everyone she had a connection with was gone. And it was all her fault.

Unshed tears formed at the corners of her eyes, and a shiver from the cold rattled her spine so hard it hurt. Self-pity was not something she could indulge in. But it was hard to ignore her circumstances when she'd spent the last month calling a ragged sleeping bag under a highway overpass home. Food was harder to come by than a decent place to sleep. The homeless shelter was half a mile away and always filled up so fast they had to turn away most of the people who showed up. They served only two meals a day with small portions since their food bank supplies remained low.

Her stomach rumbled a protest. She had to stop thinking about food.

"Damn it." She put her fist in her mouth, stumbling back into the alleyway next to the diner. The ache inside bent her over, and she wrapped her arms around her waist, hugging herself as she prayed the pain would begin to dull. Finally, it abated, briefly, and she leaned back against the brick wall of the alley, breathing slowly.

A soft scuffling was her only warning.

Zoey's eyes flew open. A man in rags and a heavy overcoat lurched toward her. A knife glinted in one hand, the blade flashing when it caught the glow from the diner.

"Hands up!" The man's rotten teeth barely showed behind his thick brown beard.

Terror seized Zoey, squeezing her lungs until she couldn't breathe. Her hands shot into the air.

"Wha…what do you want?"

"Your purse. Hand it over!" he rasped, taking one step closer.

Fear hammered against her ribs until she felt nausea and bile push their way up her throat. "I—I don't have one." She still clutched her portfolio in one hand, her fingers stinging in the cold air.

"Give me your fucking money!" His black eyes gleamed in the dim light. He could have been any of the men she'd seen at the shelter earlier today, only they were sad and broken. This man was something else. Something evil lurked in his gaze and mirrored the spark of his blade inches from her face.

"I don't have any. I have nothing…I'm sorry." Her hands shook as she took a tiny step to the side, inching away from him. Her stomach, once so desperate for food, now clenched as she struggled to control her terror.

"Don't *lie* to me! Give me what you're holding!" Flecks of spittle shot from his chapped lips as he lunged for her portfolio.

"No!" She stepped back, dropping her hands to use the portfolio as a shield.

The man held his blade with one hand and snatched at the black leather book with the other. With a cry of panic, Zoey lost her grip and the portfolio fell to the ground. Pages and photographs scattered across the snow.

"You stupid bitch!" The man snarled and dived at her.

Zoey tried to shut her eyes, but instinct kept her lids wide open. Everything slowed down. The knife slipped between her ribs inch by painful inch. He pulled the blade back out, the cold metal sharp against her flesh as he thrust it in again. Her strangled scream was drowned out by a passing bus.

Her soul seemed to coil up tight before shooting out like a firecracker, leaving her body behind. All the work, the pain, the loss of the last two years was over. Every second she'd cried, every second she'd picked herself back up, none of it mattered anymore. Her attacker pulled the blade back out and cursed before he fled into the street.

Zoey crumpled to the ground, one hand over her side. All around her the pieces of her life, the bits she'd held on to were soaking into the soil along with her blood. Hot liquid oozed through her fingers, warming them. Pain lanced through her chest with every breath. The world spun as she slid onto her back. The night sky above was lit with a smattering of faint stars, like a handful of diamonds strewn over black velvet. Her eyes burned with tears. Blood continued to pump between her loosening fingertips as she grew too weak to keep any pressure on her wounds. A tear welled up, thick and heavy, and eased down the side of her face. The trail of moisture chilled beneath the passing breeze.

Ice dug into her shoulder blades, cold and unforgiving. Invisible rocks dropped onto her chest, and a rattling noise escaped her as she fought to breathe. Her toes were numb and her arms too heavy to move. Muted laughter from people passing on the street seemed so far away. Would they see her? Did they hear her scream? Would they save her? The chill stealing over her warned her it was too late.

Too late for everything she'd never had a chance to do. A life unlived, a heart unloved, a soul alone.

Suddenly, the world around her darkened as a shape blotted out the winking stars. Glowing eyes, the color a wintery green, met her own. They pulled at her with the power of a sorcerer's spell. The sound of her favorite winter song, the "Carol of the Bells", began to echo in the air around them.

"Damn." His voice was rich and dark, a luscious baritone that made even her dying body tingle with lethargic awareness. He held one of her sketches, the white paper looked so sharp against the black sky. His eyes moved from her to the paper, some strange emotion she couldn't read flashing in his gaze.

The man looking down at her had the face of an angel, all angles and lines. His strong jaw, proud nose and bewitching eyes were framed with a halo of black hair from his head as he bent over more to look at her. The epitome of beauty. So handsome that she shivered. She truly was dying, and an angel had come for her soul.

He knelt down next to her. "I can save you. I only need you to trust me. Can you trust me?"

She tried to speak, and although her lips moved, no sound came out. Finally, she managed a jerky nod. Something deep inside her responded to his eyes. They emanated with warmth and the promise of safety shone from their depths. She trusted him.

Her angel did something unexpected. He raised his wrist to his mouth, bit into it and then put it against her mouth. She tasted blood and jerked away from his bleeding skin. A heavy scowl pulled his dark brows down.

"Poor sweetheart, just drink." The Irish lilt to his voice made her feel warm, despite the pain and the chill that threatened to consume her. Something about him, being so close…everything inside her seemed to stir to life in a way she hadn't realized she could.

A hand cupped the back of her head and held her captive while his wrist pressed deeper between her parted lips. Zoey gasped as the blood poured into her mouth and she was forced to swallow. The hand behind her head lightly massaged her scalp, the sensation wonderful and soothing. She relaxed into his gentle touch.

The tang of blood still coated the insides of her mouth when he pulled his wrist away.

"Easy, love, easy. You'll be okay now. I won't let any harm come to you." He cupped her face with his hands, his eyes fixed on hers, capturing her attention. "You will have no memory of tasting my blood. Only that you are safe, you are protected."

"Safe," she whispered. She had no memory to explain the oddly metallic taste in her mouth.

The man stroked her cheeks and nodded to himself before speaking again. "Would you let me take you home and care for you?" His earnest expression was so sharp that Zoey believed it. He wanted to help her.

"Y—yes." It was the only word she got out before she lost control of her body. Her lashes started to fan up and down and then fresh pain hit her like a freight train. She was barely aware of the man picking her up in his arms.

The sky above whirled, and the lights from the stars formed silver circles, like a cosmic Spirograph. She clamped her eyes shut as the man who held her leapt forward. The wind rushed around them, and her long hair whipped around her face but Zoey was lost in the aches surging through her body in tidal waves.

A second, an hour, a month, she wasn't sure when they stopped until she felt them grind to a halt. The pain faded, leaving her sore and bruised. She surrendered to exhaustion, hearing the man speak one last time as she let go.

"I want to keep you, little one. Keep you and never let you go."

———◆———

IAN KENNEDY STARED DOWN AT the little woman in his arms as he reached his home. She was so light and he knew she should weigh more than she did. A wee waif of a body in ragged clothes. Pity stirred in his chest like a feeble bird with injured wings.

The night was quiet in the small neighborhood where he lived. No one was watching as he slipped the key into the lock of his home and entered. A gray tabby cat lounged on the couch, watching him with silver eyes.

"Lizzy," he greeted softly. The cat let out a soft purr, her tail twitching. She was one of three strays he'd rescued in recent years, much to the frustration of his friend Connor O'Shea.

Carrying the unconscious woman into his bedroom, he eased her down onto the comforter and placed a pillow beneath her head. He grit his teeth when he leaned too close to her and the irresistible scent of blood filled his senses.

But there was more than that. Even dirty and unwashed, the scent of living on the streets didn't repel his senses as they usually did when he crossed paths with the homeless while he searched for hosts to feed from at night. A tingling ache filled his mouth, and with a low curse, he tried to stop the inevitable from happening. But he failed. Twin canine teeth extended down, ready to sink into the flesh of his prey. The flesh of the woman he'd just rescued.

Ian took a reluctant step back. Space, he needed some space or else he might give into his temptation to feed on her. She'd be out for a few hours still. He'd used his innate ability to affect her body's responses to him and gently put her to sleep. It was one of the few benefits of being a vampire.

Vampire. The word still made him cringe, but there was no point in denying what he was. He'd been alive for a hundred and ninety-five years and the older he got, the stronger his abilities seemed to become. Not only could he sway the will of most humans, he also possessed a potent ability to draw his prey to him.

This seemed to be common to all his kind. The glamour, as he liked to call it, was something every vampire possessed to some degree. Something like a pheromone, it drew human prey to them, made their victims susceptible to suggestion, to desire. And with him, it created a false sense of adoration in women. Ian rarely left the house until much later in the night to avoid being around crowds. The glamour often resulted in chaos and strange behavior.

The hollow pit in his stomach reminded him he'd been on the hunt when he'd encountered the young woman being attacked. Feeding was a priority if he was to be around her without succumbing to temptation.

It was obvious she was malnourished and needed care. And more than anything, he wanted to care for her. Too many years had passed since he'd looked upon mortals as something other than…

Shutting his eyes a brief moment, he saw flashing dark eyes, heard a woman's laugh. He'd known great love for a mortal once. Lara. His body had never felt so…human since he'd been turned. But when she'd been taken from him, he'd lost that sense of life and turned back into the predator he was.

Which is why it was so puzzling that in only an instant of seeing that woman attacked tonight, he'd needed to protect her. It was as though in her moments of terror and her dying breaths, she'd called to him—much as Lara had when he'd first met her.

With a regretful sigh at leaving the woman alone, Ian headed back outside, taking only one normal step before his body leapt into motion. The high speed of his travel, yet another one of his abilities, moved almost too fast for human sight to track. Within a minute he was in an alleyway across town, outside the diner where the woman had been wounded. The alley was empty but littered with papers. The papers from a leather portfolio lay inches from a pool of blood.

Ian knelt and began to gather the papers. Each was either a sketch or a photograph, each was captivating. He stood as he collected the binder and the last sketch. It was one of an old man, his face wrinkled, his hands gnarled as old oak tree roots clutching at a blanket as he sat on a park bench. Sadness, regret, loss of memory, all of these were locked deep into the old man's eyes. Whoever had drawn this had captured that, emotions Ian had felt every day since he'd been turned into a monster.

Something inside his chest stung and he gasped. That was odd. He'd never needed to breath before, still didn't, but his body had reacted as though it had. And the little prick of pain in his chest felt familiar, but he couldn't be sure what it was. He thumbed through the other sketches and photographs before he tucked them safely into the black binder.

"We never intervene except to feed," Connor's voice from years ago came back to him. *"The mortals must live out their lives and we cannot intercede."*

But Ian had done just that. Saved the woman from certain death. Why? He'd been moved before in the many years he'd existed like this, but there was something about her, the way she'd protected these pieces of paper as though they were her very life. The way she saw things, the details she evoked, had been a shock to his system. Jerking him out of the seemingly endless night and forcing him beneath a sun, one that didn't burn. There was only warmth here, a craving for something he lost over a hundred years ago.

A woman that made him feel like that? After so long? That was a woman he had to save, even if only to understand why she affected him like this.

"Connor will bloody kill me when he finds out," Ian muttered to himself. He glanced around. A skinny blonde-haired waitress suddenly exited the diner's backdoor in the alley to throw a large black trash bag into the dumpster. She stilled when she saw him, her eyes first widening, then slowly turning almost slumberous.

The damnable glamour was already at work. He might as well feed while the opportunity presented itself.

"Hello," she said, wiping her hands on her apron and taking a few steps toward him.

Ian tucked the portfolio into his coat and zipped it up to keep the book in place before he started toward the woman.

"Hey there, lassie," he chuckled, hiding the hint of his fangs as they slid out. A wee bite was all he needed.

THE RIVER RAN BLACK, LIKE water over obsidian, rushing away endlessly. Connor O'Shea leaned against the bridge railing watching the water. His fingertips clung to the stone, digging in hard enough that it would have ripped his skin apart if he'd been mortal. But he wasn't mortal, hadn't been for almost two centuries. Hunger beat at his insides, hunger for blood. It never ended, the urge to track and feed, to prey on humans, a constant reminder of what he no longer was.

Inside the pocket of his coat, his cell phone buzzed. He let out a low growl. It was probably Ian. The man never seemed to know when to leave him alone. Once, long ago, they'd been inseparable, as close as brothers. But they hadn't been that way for many years. Something was missing. He knew it. Ever since they'd lost their beloved Lara more than eighty years ago, he'd felt his body, his cursed soul, reverting to its monster state. He was on that slippery slope toward darker urges and he dreaded to contemplate what would happen to him, or worse what he'd do, once he stopped caring about life entirely. The words of Nietzsche regarding staring into the abyss came to mind.

If only I could jump, let the water consume me and swallow me in its depths.

But it wouldn't end things; he'd only wash up on shore somewhere and be that much hungrier.

He shook his head, trying to rid himself of the dark thoughts. In the distance, the city lights twinkled, heightened by a hint of merriness he sensed even from the many miles he was from home. Christmas time. A season he used to love. Now it filled him only with regret, with sorrow and longing…so much longing for a life he'd been robbed of. Being immortal was a curse. Time was frozen, like an old broken clock on a mantelpiece. The tiny metal arms never moved, never let time pass another second forward, and always reminded you that you did not work as you should. You did not belong.

I only want to move forward. So simple a wish, yet he knew it would not be a Christmas wish he'd ever be granted.

Santa doesn't visit vampires. He chuckled, but it was a far from merry sound. *If I saw Santa Claus, I'd likely take a bite out of the jolly old man.*

His phone vibrated again and he pulled it out. Voicemail. He hated cell phones. The damn things were such a nuisance. All the chiming, the alerts, the notifications. He hit play and put it to his ear. The message was from Ian, garbled and cut out, but the main part of the message was clear. Ian had brought home a woman for Connor to feed on, but for some reason, Ian said the woman liked to be frightened as part of the excitement. Role-play. Bah. It didn't sit well with Connor, but if the woman needed it to enjoy being fed on, well, he'd oblige her.

He stepped away from the bridge and turned his attention toward the city. Time to feed.

CHAPTER TWO

ZOEY WAS WARM. SO WARM. When was the last time she hadn't woken up to her own shivers? Weariness bled out of her, leaving only a pleasant sense of quiet, and she wondered if she was dead. There wasn't any other way to explain the sudden change in her physical surroundings. She wasn't in a hospital.

Forcing her eyelids open, it took her some time to adjust. She was lying on a massive, and incredibly soft, feather bed with a thick blanket wrapped warm and snug around her body. Like a human burrito. The thought made her giggle. She had to be dead. This had to be heaven. The last thing she remembered was the bright lights of the diner. Christmas bells ringing. The flash of a knife. Snarled words. Pain. Her heart pounded at an unsteady rhythm, and her breath quickened.

Breath? How was she breathing? And then it all came back. The man with the face of an angel and the voice of a sinner, the one who could tempt her to sell her soul for just one caress. Had he saved her? How?

Zoey's hands started to shake as she remembered blood oozing from the wounds in her chest. Fearful, she tugged the blanket down and lifted her blood-stained shirt up. The skin was clear except for two small pink slashes between her ribs. Zoey pressed her fingertips down on the marks, testing them. They were sore, but they felt like an old injury, not something that would have killed her the night before.

Suddenly remembering she was in a strange place, she looked

about the room, half hoping to find the man who'd brought her here. The bed was huge, its frame a dark wood, almost black. Despite the dimness, she could see the walls had lovely black and white photos of Paris and a few other places she thought she recognized. The crisp contrast of the photos was stunning and made her strangely homesick.

Before her life had fallen apart, she'd been studying photography. It had been her dream to live her life behind the lens, capturing moments for people. Weddings, baby showers, children's sporting matches. She wanted to capture life in vibrant colors and a contrast of grays. Nothing would have made her happier than to take photos of the events that marked the milestones in people's lives.

But that was gone, all gone. Her camera was likely still in some pawnshop collecting dust. Food and rent had been a priority, not her future. How long ago had that been? Zoey didn't want to count, but it had to be somewhere around eight months.

She sat up, pushing her hair out of her eyes, and the memories out of her head. Had the handsome guy with the Irish accent brought her here? His whispered words came back to her, the promise to keep her safe and take care of her. She vaguely recalled him asking if he could bring her home, and she'd agreed. She didn't think of herself as a weak person, but after everything she'd been through it was such a relief to think she might have help for the first time in forever.

She did feel safe. Wherever he'd taken her, she knew he wouldn't let harm come to her. It was stupid to trust a stranger, but her gut had told her to, and she'd never ignored her instincts before.

The man who'd helped her had held her tenderly, gently, as though he'd treasured her. Maybe he was like a Good Samaritan, a handsome man who stopped to save a complete stranger. If not that, he surely pitied her, enough to show her some compassion.

She didn't want anyone's pity, but it was better than apathy. She wanted to believe there were still good people out there. After everything that had happened in the last year, she was afraid to hope. But it was almost Christmas. The holidays brought the best out in people. Usually.

If only she could stay in this bed forever, wrapped in the blanket with the peaceful quiet all around her. Too many nights at the underpass had left her nervous and tense while she caught a few hours of sleep. Zoey glanced around the room, checking for a clock, but there wasn't one. The sky was gray through the blinds of the large window next to the bed. It could be evening or early morning, she couldn't tell.

Beside her on the bed lay her black portfolio. She snatched it up, wincing when her sore muscles complained. The sketches and photos were all out of order, but neatly placed back inside. She barely remembered dropping it when the man had attacked her. Her rescuer must have gone back and collected all of the pages. More than a few were dried and wrinkled in places where snow had seeped through. Hugging the portfolio to her chest a moment longer, she set it back down on the bed.

She jumped when someone knocked at the bedroom door.

"Excuse me, love. May I come in?" That beautiful, whisky rough voice. Definitely Irish.

"Uh…yes."

Her hands curled into the blanket and she raised it up to her chin. She felt oddly exposed as the man eased the door open and slid inside. Zoey craned her neck to look up at him. He had to be at least six-three, with black hair long enough to touch the collar of his shirt and a thin layer of stubble. He looked like a pirate off the cover of a romance novel. His white shirtsleeves were rolled up to reveal muscled forearms, and the two top buttons were undone below his throat. She was struck by how large he was. His shoulders alone were massive. She had the sudden urge to touch them, feel the strength of the muscles beneath her palm. Her mouth ran dry as a quickening in her blood made her feel light-headed. He was a stranger; why did she want to suddenly kiss him? It made no sense at all.

"How are you doing?" He came to the bed and raised a hand to her forehead. His skin was cold, shockingly so, and she flinched from the contact. The man's face paled and he pulled back. "Sorry about that."

"It's okay. Just…cold." Even though she didn't want to be cold again, she'd suffer it just to have his hand back on her forehead. The whisper of a secret thrill skated along her skin, and already she missed his touch.

The man turned away and flicked on the lamp on her nightstand. The wash of gold light illuminated her mysterious rescuer. His face was just as beautiful as she'd remembered. Sharp angles and masculine perfection highlighted by dark brows above piercing winter green eyes. Faint lines bracketed his mouth as though he smiled often.

She met his gaze with a shy smile. Men like him never glanced her way, not even out of pity. Ever since she'd lost her home, she'd become almost invisible to the world. Especially men. A blush flooded her cheeks when she realized how she must look to him. Hair unwashed in thick oily strands, blood staining her flannel shirt and mud-stained jeans.

"Oh God, I must have ruined your bed!" She struggled to get free of the blanket and flopped like a fish over the edge. She braced herself for impact, but his arms shot out and caught her. She was pulled up and trapped against his upper body in a gentle embrace.

"Careful, love." His eyes glittered with mischief. "Now, about your stomach. It's been grumbling for the last several hours. How about I fix it for you?"

Zoey blinked, unsure of what he meant.

He smiled. "I could go out and get something for you to eat?"

"That's really not necessary. I…I should go." But she really wanted him to let her stay. At least for another hour. Long enough for her to preserve some warmth before facing the cold again.

He shook his head. "No. You're not leaving." His voice brooked no argument.

Zoey clamped her lips shut, happy not to argue. It was probably unwise to stay with a stranger, even a handsome one. But she needed a day, at least one day away from the cold. But she couldn't forget his promise—she was safe with him. And as silly as it was, she believed it.

He strode to the door with her still tucked firmly in his arms. "Let me get you settled on the couch. Unless you'd like to wash first?"

Zoey must have made a noise, something to indicate how desperately she wanted a hot shower, because his chest shook with silent laughter.

"A shower it is, then." He changed directions and headed down another hallway. He released her legs, letting her stand while he opened the bathroom door. A large glass shower stall was in the corner, and an even larger whirlpool tub was next to it.

She started to walk to the tub. "Oh, wow." Maybe she wanted a bath first—a good long soak would be better.

"What's your name?" The man's question distracted her. She spun on her heel, shocked to find him shutting the door, sealing them both in the bathroom.

"Zo…" She swallowed, her mouth suddenly dry. "Zoey Blake."

He extended his hand and she placed her palm in his. "A pleasure to meet you, Zoey. I'm Ian Kennedy. I live here with my friend Connor O'Shea and three cats, Titus, Cleo and Lizzy."

Three cats? And a roommate? Maybe her fallen angel wasn't into women. That would be just her luck. To be rescued by a god among men and find he was more interested in his roommate.

"Thank you for bringing me here, Ian." She hesitated before finally asking what had been nagging at the back of her mind. "I was attacked by a man in that alley. I know I was hurt pretty badly. What happened? I remember you helping me…but…" She needed him to explain how she'd magically healed from something that should have killed her. The details of that were still fuzzy. The only thing she remembered was her lips on his wrist and feeling safe with him.

"That's an interesting story," he began, but her stomach interrupted. "I'll tell you after you've cleaned up and gotten some food in you." He winked at her.

"But—"

Ian placed a finger over her lips, a quick smile flitting past his face, giving him a boyish charm. It also made her insides hum to life.

"Shower, food, and then we'll talk. Deal?"

She agreed, albeit reluctantly.

"Good." Ian reached for the top button of her shirt. Before she could stop them, her hands shot up, fingers curling around his wrists. She looked up at him from beneath her lashes. Even though his fingers were cold, whenever they brushed her skin an electric shock jolted her more awake. She wanted that jolt, that kick to her system more than she wanted to shower or eat. The blood in her body pumped through her wild and hard enough to rush against her ear drums.

Ian undid the first button of her shirt. Slow and methodical, he proceeded to undo the others.

"I…" His voice was hoarse. "I'll get you something to wear. Go ahead and hop in the shower." He released the edges of her shirt and turned away, exiting the bathroom. He didn't shut the door behind him.

Zoey stared at the open door for several seconds before she came back to herself. A shower! She wanted to strip off her clothes and rush in, but she took her time, enjoying this as much as possible. There was no telling when she'd have the chance to bathe in hot water again. She toed off her black Converse shoes, peeled off her socks, unzipped her ragged jeans and slipped out of her underwear.

Looking over her shoulder at her reflection in the mirror, she flinched. Her body was covered in grime. Weeks of dirt and muck covered her skin. With a shiver of revulsion, she turned back to the shower and reached for the polished chrome knobs. She cranked them hard, hot as they could go and waited until steam curled up from the gray tile floor. She stepped inside, sliding the glass door closed behind her.

The water burned. It felt so good, like heaven. She let the scalding spray wash away the dirt, but she felt something deeper inside being cleaned. The chill in her bones gradually vanished as she rubbed the masculine-scented body wash over her limbs. She couldn't help but think of Ian, rubbing his hands over her body.

Once she was squeaky clean, she turned to her hair, lathering it with the shampoo and then the conditioner.

There was a single razor sitting on a shelf on the back wall of the shower. It was a large masculine thing but Zoey snatched it up anyway. She wanted to look her best for Ian and smooth legs and underarms would help. When she'd finished, she simply stood beneath the spray, soaking further in the heat.

And then she started to cry.

Sobs choked out of her, fat tears leaked out and she rubbed her fists against her closed eyelids, trying to banish them. Exhausted, she leaned forward, resting her head against the marble, eyes closed as she breathed in slow, ragged breaths.

Her body hurt. Her chest expanded as she sucked in air and a twinge of pain came back to her. She touched her smooth unmarred stomach and chest again, trying not to think too hard about how she'd been miraculously healed. The faint pink scars she'd seen a short while ago were only pale pink lines. Relief followed the tears as she regained control of herself. She was safe, warm and clean. It was something to be happy about, even if it didn't last more than a day.

The shower door behind her slid open, a trickle of cold air teased her, making her turn around. Ian stood just outside the shower, his jaw clenched.

Zoey could barely breathe. His gaze raked over her. Heat flooded her face, and she looked away. It had been over a year since she'd been naked in front of a man. She was naturally a little shy, but there was something about the way he looked at her that made her feel vulnerable, a feeling she liked.

Everything about this situation should have freaked her out. Did he want to have sex with her? Did he expect her to sleep with him because he'd saved her and brought her home? If that was what he wanted…she was afraid to tell him no. He held all the power here. He'd given her shelter, a shower, had promised food. Was she going to barter her body for the comforts she'd been deprived of for so many months?

Take a deep breath, she told herself. *I'm in a strange man's house, and he is gazing at my naked body with heated interest.* That should scare the hell out of her, and it did… but it was also exciting. She wanted more. She wanted his hungry gaze on her, his gentle hands exploring her. Someone to care about her, even just a little bit, even just for a little while. As long as he was gentle, kind, and made her feel alive and warm and excited then she wouldn't feel forced.

"Zoey." He caressed her name, yet she could read the concern in those eyes. "I heard crying. Are you okay?"

She slicked her wet hair back from her face, then dropped her arms to curl around her waist.

"I'm fine. I just… I'm sorry." She didn't know why she was apologizing. It didn't seem to matter. He was gazing at her mouth, a look of starvation on his face, one she knew only too well. With slow, measured actions, he stripped out of his clothes until he wore nothing but black boxers.

"Ian?" she whispered, a little anxious as he stepped inside and slid the door closed again, sealing them together in the intimate, steamy confines of the shower. Even as her mind cautioned her that he was a stranger, her body stirred to life in anticipation in a way she hadn't in a long time.

"Let me kiss you. Just one kiss. I want to remember… It's been so long." Ian dropped his head until his forehead rested against hers. His hands came up to cup her face, his thumbs pressed against her cheeks.

Passion built up inside her like a warm, dark cloud. One that fogged her mind with visions of twining limbs, whispered sighs and sated pleasures. She needed this one kiss too, more than Ian did.

"Okay."

He lifted her chin and put his mouth over hers. It was a spark to tinder, and she went up in flames. A wildfire raged between their lips. More. She had to have more. It was crazy, insane, but she gave in and arched her body into his. His hands moved from her face down to her waist, sliding over slick skin. His palms slid up her back then down to her butt. His thumbs pressed into the flare of the front of her hips, his fingers dug into her lower back, pulling her closer. He feathered his lips, soft and fleeting before she whimpered in frustration. This was no time for teasing. A breathless chuckle escaped Ian as he spun them around to pin her against the marble wall of the shower.

His mouth assaulted hers, taking everything she gave him and demanding still more. He moaned when his tongue slid between her parted lips, tangling in fierce play. The hot spray of the shower struck Ian's shoulders, thick droplets formed over his skin and Zoey fought the desire to lean forward and lick them away.

At some point, her legs were lifted and parted. Ian's hands grabbed the back of her thighs. He pulled her up until her breasts were level with his mouth. She gasped in shock as his lips settled over one peak, sucking hard on the tender, erect tip. Her legs wrapped around his waist as she clung to him. Zoey's eyes fell shut as bliss began to pulse and throb between her legs, the almost forgotten rhythm wild and frantic. She rubbed herself against him and the massive erection barely hidden by his boxers.

She jerked in his arms when Ian's teeth grazed over her other nipple, pricking the sensitive skin.

She squeaked when he nipped at the underside of her breast. The zing of pain only made her throb harder and her core filled with her wet arousal.

Ian growled. His tongue flitted over one nipple before his mouth moved back up her chest to her neck. He nuzzled the side of her throat, teeth scraping over skin. His soft inhalation of breath was an erotic whisper.

"You smell so good, Zoey, love. I can feel your heat…" His words trailed off into a gruff curse when her stomach rumbled loudly. Ian sighed, resting his cheek against her collarbone.

Finally, he leaned back and let her slide down his body until her feet hit the floor.

Her body wanted to scream in frustration at being denied his touch, his kiss. "Why'd you stop?"

"I'm sorry, Zoey. I took advantage and it was wrong of me." His hands seemed reluctant to part with her waist, but he turned his face away, eyes roving about the bathroom, as though determined to stay away from her. He was panting, apparently struggling to regain control.

His apparent desire to put distance between them, to take back what they'd done, hurt her more than countless days of hunger or cold. What he'd given her had been so wonderful. A glimpse of unbridled passion and a sensual exploration she'd never had the chance for until now. And he'd taken it all away with a well-intended apology.

"Please don't say that. I…I liked it." She couldn't believe she felt comfortable enough admitting it. She followed her brave words with the cowardly action of wrapping her arms around her chest, hiding her breasts. His gaze moved back to her face and she was struck again by the lovely green of his eyes. She'd never seen such a pure color. She'd have happily stared into those eyes forever and never want anything more, except for another kiss. She'd sell her soul and bargain away her heart for a touch of those lips on hers.

"I know. But it was wrong. You don't owe me anything. You're free to stay here until…until we can get you back on your feet. I'll leave something on the counter for you to wear. Don't worry if I'm gone when you get out. Settle on the couch and rest up a bit."

He cupped her chin and leaned down for a kiss, and it was anything but chaste. How could he pack so much erotic promise in one little kiss?

When he stepped back, her body screamed in protest, but she didn't stop him as he slid open the shower door and stepped out. Water pooled around his large feet onto the small bath rug. He reached behind himself and closed the shower door, putting the fogged glass between them as he strode away.

The corners of her mouth pulled up in a smile. Ian. She liked him more than she should and she didn't know him at all. Except that he could kiss like a dream and not just on her mouth. Her cheeks flamed and she stifled a breathless giggle as she remembered the way he'd fit his mouth to her breasts, sucking and tugging on each nipple with hungry insistence. Each pull on her breast sent a trail of fire straight to her clit. The memory had her aching all over again.

Frustrated, she washed between her legs, but it wasn't much use; she stayed aroused as she stepped out of the shower. She toweled off and blinked in shock when she noticed the folded white shirt sitting on the counter. Surely, he brought something else to wear. Why hadn't he brought pants?

Zoey buried her face in her hands, massaged her cheeks and sucked in a deep breath before blowing it out. She'd practically had sex with Ian in the shower. Maybe her reaction to him gave him the impression she was easy. She was mortified about how her inner moral compass seemed quite happy to ignore all this. Searching the drawers for a comb, she found a black brush instead, and quickly untangled her wet hair.

Clean. Finally clean. It felt so damn wonderful. This time, when she raised her eyes to the mirror, she saw herself. A plain Jane with chestnut hair and brown eyes. But at least it was her, not some homeless, grimy, smelly creature. No one really understood what it was like to lose themselves to a life on the streets. A person lost their identity when they lost their home, work, money, and family. All of it had vanished in a year and it had changed her forever. Yet now she could glimpse Zoey Blake again, even if her face was a little gaunt, her eyes a little sunken. She was still there somewhere.

Zoey picked up the white shirt left on the counter and slid her arms into the sleeves. It had to be one of Ian's. It hung down to her mid-thighs and her hands vanished in the long sleeves. She rolled them up until she could find her wrists. Outside the bathroom, she heard a distant door slam.

"Ian!" Her heart leapt as she ran to the open the bathroom door. Her smile vanished when she stared up into another man's face. Just as attractive, yet the opposite of Ian, with golden hair and dark eyes, looking more innocent. Yet Zoey could tell he was far from that. Something kicked her hard, raw animal desire for this complete stranger… It was just like when she'd first watched Ian cross the bedroom and come to her—an irresistible need to kiss him, to curl her arms around his neck and offer herself to him in every wicked way she desired. Vaguely she realized something was wrong with her, if she was reacting so irrationally to these two strangers.

The man's lips parted, and he snarled, his canines long and menacing, like fangs.

"Such a succulent feast for dinner? Ian shouldn't have…" The man licked his lips and reached for her.

CHAPTER THREE

Z OEY COULDN'T EVEN SUMMON A scream. The man was like some kind of Viking warrior with bronzed gold hair and honey brown eyes that promised wicked sins and wild abandon. His lips peeled back in a feral smile that reminded her of those old Bela Lugosi vampire movies. His massive shoulders blocked any exit from the bathroom and his dilated pupils forced her to step back. An unexpected wave of desire swept through her to run her hands up the length of his chest, digging her nails into him while she kissed a path up to his mouth.

"You're not Ian," managed to come out of her mouth, though barely above a croaked whisper.

"Sorry to disappoint. He brought you here for me. I promise once we get started you won't miss him." The man's face, while handsome, was somehow cold and frightening. His eyes stilled her in place like a frightened hare coming face to face with a timber wolf. Even though she was afraid, she still had that ridiculous urge to jump into his arms and beg for a kiss.

What is wrong with me?

"Please don't…" Zoey wasn't sure what she was asking, but anything else she might have said was silenced when the man seized her and jerked her into him. She collided with his broad chest, feeling the hard muscles against her breasts through the thin protection of his shirt and hers.

"Let me kiss you, love. Just say no if you don't want a taste." He licked his lips.

She knew she should deny him, but she wanted that kiss, as stupid and illogical as it was.

She nodded. "Yes."

One large palm moved up to hold her by the back of her neck as he dropped his head, taking her mouth with his. His other moved down her back to shape the curve of her ass. He clenched it tight as he bit her bottom lip and invaded her mouth.

Her body went off like a pail full of Black Cat fireworks. She couldn't contain the moan of pure drugged pleasure and the wild urge to let him do whatever he wished to her. His tongue dueled with hers for dominance, and she quickly, willingly surrendered. When he coaxed her to enter his mouth, her tongue flicked against his fangs.

The fog that flooded her brain when he'd started to kiss her was temporarily penetrated with a beam of clarity, like sunlight streaking through morning mist. He had fangs… She should be afraid that he was…was…what was he? Zoey fisted her hands now trapped against his chest and tried to push him back. She failed. He growled against her lips and then released her. His chest moved with rapid breaths and for some reason that eased her mind, if only for a second.

"You want to be scared? I can scare you." His voice had lost its gruffness. He was all silk and seduction now.

She leaned one hand against the bathroom counter, trying to steady herself. Her legs insisted on buckling after that mind–numbing kiss. "What?"

"Run," he snarled. "Run and hide or I'll rip your pretty little throat out!"

Light gleamed against the stark white of his fangs and Zoey didn't hesitate. She shoved past him and fled the bathroom. Her instincts finally took over and shook off the remnants of that insane arousal he'd spiked her body into moments before. She bolted down the hall toward the front door but he was suddenly there at the far end of the room, arms crossed, blocking the door.

"That's not how this game works, pet. You run, I catch you. Then I feed and we fuck."

Zoey stared at him from across the room as she tried to process his words.

"Feed and…" She couldn't bring herself to say the other word. It was so coarse, so raw, so…primal. She was torn between fear of what his fangs suggested and desire for what he was offering. Sleeping with him would be beyond anything she'd ever experienced. The riotous shivers rippling through her weren't from terror, but pure lust.

The man cocked one eyebrow and gestured for her to move. "Run. Now."

She didn't understand what was happening, or why he was doing this to her but she didn't want to stick around and find out. It was obvious her body was ready to betray her and encourage her to sleep with both this man and Ian. However, that was not what her brain wanted her to do so she had to escape before he got too close again. That sexy mojo he seemed to ooze that made her unable to think past her libido.

There were other rooms, rooms that had windows. If she could just get to one and get outside, she'd find someone to call for help. Zoey picked the first door she came to and slammed it shut behind her. She flicked the lock into place. She darted over to the window and shoved up against the window sill. It didn't budge. She hissed in frustration, fists smacking against the glass. There wasn't time to bust through the window. Zoey whirled around, hastily scanning the room. Hiding under the bed? Not an option. The closet? Also not an option. She stared at the locked door and her heart leapt into her throat, lodging there as the knob jiggled.

"Come on, pet. Don't make me break the door. It is *my* bedroom after all," the man on the other side teased. He had an Irish accent as well. Was this Ian's friend Connor? She hoped not. Otherwise she'd have to warn Ian his friend was…was a…

"Okay, I'm losing it," she muttered. "He can't be a vampire. That's just ridiculous." Her eyes zeroed in on the still jiggling doorknob.

The man chuckled low from the other side of the door. "Not as ridiculous as you think."

Zoey gasped. The knob suddenly stopped moving, and the lock slowly twisted. She threw herself at the door, hands gripping the lock, fighting to keep it in place. It was a battle she knew she'd lose, even as her fingers screamed against the metal, biting into it as the door pushed inward.

"No!" She dug in her heels, using her body's weight to keep the door shut, but the man simply knocked it open. Zoey stumbled backward and fell against the large bed. The man stood in the doorway, the light from the hall turning him into an ominous silhouette of strength and danger.

"Scared enough?" His question caught her off guard but when he advanced another step, she screamed.

She scrambled backward over the comforter, sinking deep into the downy softness, giving him all the time he needed to pounce. He gripped her ankles and tugged. She fell onto her back as he dragged her toward him. Ian's large white shirt rode up to her hips and she thrashed, fighting for her life. She expected him to force her legs apart and mount her.

He didn't.

Instead, he drew her legs together, his touch tender but firm, winding one arm around her calves and holding her still as he climbed onto the bed next to her. Zoey pushed up on her elbows, breathing hard as he leaned over her. She wasn't sure how long they stared at each other. The room was dark but his eyes seemed to channel what little light there was. The burnt sienna depths ensnared her, held her prisoner. His palm tightened on her calves and then after a moment loosened.

He slid his hand up her outer left thigh under the dress shirt. "I don't like it when you're afraid of me," he whispered. "Ian said to scare you, but…I don't care for it." He seemed to be talking to himself more than her. "The last thing I want is to frighten you or take you against your will." His words cut through the rising fear and instead brought back that insane arousal she didn't understand.

"Tell me now, little one, do you not want me to touch you?"

The hand beneath her shirt moved in slow circles over her hip, then her belly, his fingers drifting closer to her mound. Her entire body surrendered to the violent shaking that rippled through her. The gentle sensuality of his touch thrilled her, and the fear that had mounted in her seemed to ebb away. He didn't want to scare her. Maybe he didn't want to hurt her either.

"I…I don't *not* want you to touch me," she admitted, unable to actually say she wanted him. It was close enough, and the way his eyes glittered, she knew he understood what she meant. She remembered something he'd said earlier. "Scare me? Why would Ian want to scare me?" Where she'd found the strength to speak, she didn't know.

He chuckled, his breath teasing her hair as he brushed his lips over her ear lobe. "Some women like a bit of fear." His teeth grazed her neck. "Heightens their pleasure." His tongue flicked against her skin. "But I don't want you scared, I want you *hot*."

The word came out a soft growl and she was ready to surrender everything to him in that moment. It was wild and insane and she wanted him, was tempted by him. No man had ever made her feel this crazy, except Ian. Ian! She'd lusted after him before and now she was craving this other man's touch. It was madness and she knew it, but she didn't want to fight it any longer.

The man's hand drifted between her thighs, one finger finding her clit and pressing. She arched off the bed right into him.

"There now, see? We don't need fear," the man whispered a second before he licked the shell of her ear. Sharp tingles of violent pleasure electrified her spine and she whimpered.

"You…you're not going to hurt me?" She eased onto her back and he followed her down, his mouth doing wicked things below her ear. His hand between her thighs began to play. His fingers parted the slick folds of her sex and stroked lazy patterns into her burning center. It was so hard to think, to speak, she just wanted him to take her, now, to bring her to a burning explosion so she could forget about everything but him.

"No, pet. I won't hurt you, but you may feel a sting."

His fangs sank into her neck. The pain was unexpected, but the pleasure that followed was even more of a surprise. Her hands found his biceps, and she curled her fingers into his skin as she held on for dear life, riding the building waves of pleasure from the bite and his touch. His mouth worked at her neck, sucking as he drank, but she couldn't find it in herself to care. He'd said he wouldn't hurt her. As foolish as it was, she trusted him. Just like she'd trusted Ian.

The man parted her core with two fingers and thrust them inside in a slow rhythm that gradually built in speed. She circled her hips against his hand, urging him deeper. She needed more.

"Please…" she gasped and wound one hand through his long, dark blond hair.

When he didn't respond, she tugged sharply. He lifted his head. Blood stained his lips a deep red and his tongue flicked out, swiping the blood away. His warm eyes were wreathed in crimson, and his fangs now gleamed lean and dangerous from behind the curve of his sensual lips.

Clarity cleared his gaze and he started moving his hand faster, his fingers pumping harder, deeper. He added a third finger and she screamed. Something detonated inside her, lighting her up like the stars in the winter sky. She imploded, all sense of self vanishing. She was in ecstasy.

A distant crash invaded her cloud of hazy delight and the man leapt off her. Zoey blinked, trying to focus her blurry vision on another, someone standing in the doorway.

"Zoey! Zoey, love, are you hurt?"

Ian.

"I'm uh…I don't know…Ian…" She hesitated, looking at the scowling form of Connor lingering at the edge of the doorway. "He…He's a vampire. That guy is a vampire."

Ian closed his eyes, drew a deep breath.

"I know."

She tensed with apprehension. "You know?"

Ian bit his bottom lip as though embarrassed. She saw the tips of two fangs peek out of Ian's mouth. Her jaw dropped.

"We both are."

CHAPTER FOUR

IAN WAS A VAMPIRE? THEY both were? Zoey blinked, her brain short circuiting as she tried to process this information and failed.

"Oh my God. He bit me! Am I going to turn into one?"

Ian was suddenly above her, his hands on her neck, her legs, everywhere as he checked her for injury.

"No, lass, no. You won't become a vampire. That takes more than just a bite to accomplish."

Relief surged through her. She wasn't going to go Bela Lugosi after all.

"Connor, you damned fool. What are you doing biting her?"

Connor, she'd been right to assume it was him, shifted uneasily by the door, his blond hair still wild from her hands running through it.

"You left me a message. Said she was my dinner and I had to scare her."

"What? That's not what I said, you *amadan!*" Ian scooped Zoey up into his arms. She burrowed into him instinctively. The remnants of her climax still rippled through her and his strong arms absorbed her trembling.

"Ian…" Connor growled.

"I said I had a guest and was bringing her dinner. I warned you to be sure *not* to scare her. Bloody hell man, she'll never forgive me. Not after you attacked her."

Ian carried her to the living room and settled her on the leather couch. He grabbed a heavy thick blanket and tucked it around her. Connor followed at a distance, his eyes avoiding Zoey's. That irritated her, not that she could say why exactly.

"Ian, I'm sorry. The message cut out in places. I thought I heard what I heard. I didn't know. It's clear she's your dinner. I didn't realize you were bringing them home again. You usually eat out."

Ian, who had been brushing hair back from Zoey's face, tensed. His eyes caught hers and held them for a time before he spoke to Connor.

"She's not my dinner. She's a woman who's in need of some help. I offered her a place to stay and to get her some food." He pointed to the kitchen countertop, which had several take-out bags from the nearby restaurants.

The scent of the food drifted beneath Zoey's nose. Her mouth watered. Hunger hit her stomach like a physical blow. Food. God, she was ravenous. She'd quite forgotten it when she'd been beneath Connor on his bed.

Her eyes strayed to the kitchen where the food was. It took every ounce of self-control not to run straight at it. Somehow she felt making sudden movements in front of a pair of vampires was a bad idea.

Vampires. She still had to process that, but she could do that later, when her stomach was full.

"Who is she, Ian?"

Ian lifted her up and sat back on the couch with her in his lap. "Her name is Zoey Blake."

It probably should have bothered her that he just moved her about and picked her up without asking. But she liked that he simply took control—and more importantly, that he seemed to enjoy keeping her close. Even with the allure of food so nearby she was reluctant to leave his arms.

Connor's eyes narrowed to slits. "And *why* did you bring Zoey here?"

The air about them seemed to vibrate, like someone had just plucked the strings of a harp and the sound waves still traveled along the air. The hair on Zoey's neck rose and her skin tingled with awareness of the two men and the situation.

"She has nowhere else to go. The lass lost her family, her home. I found her dying in an alley where some whoreson had attacked her." Ian's voice was full of quiet desperation, but tinged with an edge of defiance.

Connor's lips twisted. "So you thought you'd bring her home and play nursemaid? What about your promise to me? No more mortal lovers. Not after what happened to Lara."

Zoey stiffened. Mortal lover? "Who's Lara?" She glanced up at Ian. The movement brushed her lips across the line of his jaw. He tensed, chest and arm muscles hardening. The sudden bulge she felt beneath her had her blushing.

"You test me, love. Be careful." Ian's warm breath stirred the crown of her hair, eliciting small shivers from her. "Connor, she stays. Get used to the idea. She's mine, and I will care for her. You are welcome to help, but do not make me choose between you. I will pick her. We swore once to protect the innocent. Zoey is as innocent as they come."

"Hey! I'm not that innocent." Zoey was no stranger to sex— assuming that's what he meant. There had been a few boys in college before she was forced to drop out, and even if it had been a few years, she still remembered the mechanics of it. Even if she'd been involuntarily celibate lately, she'd still held her share of wicked fantasies, her current one featuring the pair of men both arguing about her.

Connor snorted. "You're as green as the grass near Belfast."

"I'm not sure what that means," Zoey shot back, a tad uncertain but still riled enough to glower at him. "But I think I'm insulted."

Ian chuckled, but it died once she glared at him with all the fury a woman could muster, which seemed to be enough to make his eyes twinkle despite his lack of a smile. She turned her glower to Connor, hoping to have a better effect.

"Don't argue with me, pet," Connor growled. "I'm liable to turn you over my knee and smack your arse until it's red."

"You're not to touch her." Ian shielded her with his arms, but she wasn't scared. Connor's threat had her body heating, and the promise of his hand on her ass, even in punishment, melted her insides. God, she needed help. This was so wrong. She shouldn't want him to spank her, and it sure as hell shouldn't have aroused her.

Connor turned his back on them and slammed his hands down on the granite kitchen countertop. His head dropped between his hunched shoulders.

"Connor?"

Tension rolled off Connor's back in waves. She couldn't help but remember what happened minutes before when he'd had her on her back. There hadn't been any tension there, only passion. Her surrender, his domination, and a release the likes of which she'd never felt before. Her womb clenched at the memory of his fingers pumping inside her. Then she remembered she was in Ian's arms. She raised her head and saw his nostrils flaring. Surely he couldn't…*smell* her arousal?

God, I hope not.

"She's helpless, Connor. I refuse to put her back out onto the streets."

Connor turned back to face them. "Another stray, like your cats. But you can't keep her, Ian. She's a human, not a wee animal."

Ian's shoulders stiffened. A low growl emanated from his throat. Zoey's hackles rose, and she realized that Ian was just as dangerous as Connor, although he'd hidden it from her with his outward gentleness.

As the thought filtered through her hungry mind, she felt a sudden stab of anger, and the prickling of tears behind her eyes. Why hadn't she seen it before? She would have, she argued to herself, if she hadn't been so hungry.

Ian didn't look at her with passion—he looked at her with pity. She'd mistaken his intentions in the bathroom earlier when he'd kissed her. Men did that, didn't they? Sleep with women they pitied?

The pain of that thought wracked her insides with an angry sadness that choked her. Zoey was too angry to say a word. Emotions ripped through her and she didn't dare open her mouth;

otherwise she'd say a thousand things she'd regret.

Connor looked away. "You should have let nature run its course. We cannot save every mortal we come across."

"Let nature run its course?" Ian's reply was barely comprehensible as it came out in a vicious snarl. "Do you remember when nature ran its course back in Ireland? Our families starved, our people died on the streets, like the very animals I try to save. How dare you hold that against me, against her!"

She couldn't stand to be there a second longer. She had to leave. Zoey shoved at Ian's chest. Whatever was going on between these two, she didn't understand it, and she didn't want to. She was too hurt by Ian's words. A stray? No better than a starving cat on the streets? That's how he saw her? A thing to be pitied, not a person to be loved?

Ian fought her for only a second before he let her go. Somehow, that made everything worse. She bit back a fresh well of tears.

He didn't even care enough to fight to keep her in his arms. It stung—no, it burned—like a knife sliding between her ribs and piercing her heart.

Zoey slid off the couch, her bare feet sinking into the soft thick carpet. She had to tug Ian's white dress shirt down to cover her bare thighs. Both men stared at her, their gazes drawn to her legs.

"Ian. Where are my clothes?" She said it softly, but he heard her.

The confusion on his face would have been endearing at any other time, but the tension in the room was thick enough to smother her.

"Why do you need your clothes?" Ian's face was a mirror image of the brooding Connor on the other side of the room.

"I think I should leave. You both clearly have things you need to discuss, and I don't want to be in the way."

"No!" Ian barked. "Absolutely not."

Zoey flinched, but held her ground. "I'm sorry, I can't stay. I don't want your pity…" Her voice trailed off, face flushing when she realized she'd wanted something else. Him. When her eyes strayed to Connor, something hit her in the gut. As frightening as he was, she had to admit he fascinated her as well. When it had been just the two of them alone in his bed, he'd chosen not to scare her, but instead to overwhelm her with raw passion. She'd been a moth to the fire of his embrace.

She wanted Connor. She wanted Ian. It was insane to want them both, yet she did. They were immortal creatures, vampires. *Vampires*. She still hadn't fully processed this. Eventually she'd have a hell of a headache when she had to accept that fact. But she wasn't going to think about that right now, not when she had to figure out what she was going to do and where she was going to go. She was still homeless. A stray. They didn't want her, they only pitied her.

Zoey raised her chin, trying to think of all of the things she should be proud of, and not let her own self-pity weigh her down. If she left now, she might make it to the shelter before they closed and maybe, just maybe they'd have space for her in the main room, rather than having to go back to the underpass.

A shudder of fear tinged with anxiety shot up her spine. Another horrible night under that concrete bridge…hoping no one would attack her. It had happened before. Hands groping in the darkness, trapping her limbs, fetid breath on her face, rags shoved inside her mouth to prevent her from screaming while an accomplice stole what little food she'd kept for when she needed it. That was what she had to look forward to.

"You can't go, love. Please." Ian's tone was heavy, but his fists were clenched and his taut expression revealed surprising determination.

"I won't be an object of pity, Ian. Besides…" She pointed at Connor. "He doesn't want me here."

A storm cloud hovered over Ian's features as he turned back to his friend. "I don't give a damn what you think, Connor. I'm keeping her. So apologize to the lass. If you won't, I'll take you outside and beat you until you do."

The threat was delivered with no hint of the gentlemanly front Ian had shown her up to now. This was an animal establishing his dominance where a female was concerned. Recognizing this for what it was made Zoey shiver with forbidden desire. She shouldn't like the idea of Ian being possessive, but she did.

In another place and time, Connor's scowl might have made Zoey laugh. He looked like a spoiled child who was being told "no" for the first time. She had a feeling he got his way more often than not when they quarreled. Finally, his expression changed to one of stony defiance.

"Fine. She can stay. For now."

That was all he said. No apology, no negotiation. Just a gruff reply before he stalked from the room.

Zoey winced when he slammed the door to his bedroom. He'd shut her out, but it felt like more than that. Why that mattered, she was too afraid to consider. She didn't want to contemplate that she was crushing on a vampire…make that *two* vampires. She remembered the way he'd pleasured her, the way it felt to be powerless and yet feel so safe with him.

Ian's voice broke through her thoughts. "Zoey."

She raised her eyes and saw him leaning against the side of the couch, his green eyes dark with concern. He closed the distance between them so he could cup her chin with one hand. Sparks tingled from that single point of contact, making her flush with heat.

"I don't pity you. Never think that. But I do want to help, and I need you to stay. Please." There was desperation in his voice that filled his every syllable. It made her feel guilty for denying him something he needed.

She reached up and curled her fingers around his strong wrist. "Why do you need to help me?" She didn't pull his hand away, merely kept hold of him, like a grounding rod to attract the lightning strikes his gentle yet possessive touch seemed to bring.

His thumb traced her lips, his eyelids dropped to half-mast as he gazed at her mouth.

"Connor and I are best friends. We grew up in the same village in Ireland. We watched our friends and loved ones die during the Great Famine over a hundred and fifty years ago. It…" His voice grew hoarse and soft. "It ruined me, ruined us both. We were turned into immortals against our will. I remember…hearing Connor shouting and begging to die. I was too weak to cry out…I screamed in my head, but it didn't stop the pain, or the blood from flowing from that creature's wrist to my mouth. A little blood would have saved me, but the creature drained me and turned me. Made me one of them. I hated that I was helpless."

"You gave me your blood…I remember now." She licked her lips, the memory of that horrible moment came rushing back.

Ian's eyes darkened to sharp slices of jade. "Only enough to heal you from your wounds. I wouldn't have taken the choice of life or immortality away from you the way it had been taken from me."

She could see in his face that this meant something to him. The choice to be what he was. Immortal.

"Thank you for saving me. I didn't really say that before…"

He grinned. "You were in shock, love. And you're welcome. I will admit to selfish reasons though. I wanted to take you home with me."

As sweet as his words were, Zoey couldn't let herself read too much into it, not when she might get her hopes up for something that could never be. She tried to change the subject back to the story of his turning. "What happened after you changed?"

"I was condemned, as was Connor. We both swore we'd never let another creature suffer the way we had, the way our families had. When I found you, it was like I was mortal again, watching my sister starve to death. I had to save you."

Jealous pain cut through Zoey's chest. She didn't want him to think of her as his sister. Not after the way he'd kissed her. A sense of grief flooded through her as she absorbed his words. His sister had starved. Zoey knew how terrible that fate was. But the fact was she couldn't remain here with them.

"Connor's right, Ian. I can't stay here. Not forever."

"So stay awhile. Let me care for you until you can get back on your feet."

It was so tempting. She wanted to say yes, to agree to anything he asked. He was a dream, a wonderful and strange one. Maybe she had died in that alley after all, and the afterlife was nothing more than this, a dream that she'd be teased and tormented with for the rest of eternity.

Promises of a life I'll never live.

"Okay. I'll stay for a while. But once I'm ready to leave, you have to let me go."

Ian nodded soberly and stood. He walked over to the kitchen bar and started opening the bags of take-out sitting there.

"Shall we feed you before it gets cold? I have fried rice, tacos, cheeseburgers and pasta. What would you like?"

She heard the false cheer in his tone. He was hurt, but so was she. At least she could have some food as consolation. She forced a smile.

"Can I have a little bit of everything?"

Genuine warmth twinkled behind his eyes as Ian flashed a grin. "Finally, something I can do."

He grabbed some dishes from the cabinets and started digging food out of the bags.

She suddenly recalled they'd mentioned a woman named Lara. She focused on it rather than her hunger pangs. "Will you tell me about her?"

"Who?" Ian asked.

"Lara. I want to know about her."

Ian blew out a slow breath as he closed the cabinets, his hand on the silver knob, hesitating before he spoke.

"Lara was a dream. More fantasy than reality I think sometimes. I met her in 1923 and fell hard for her. So did Connor. My father would have called her one of the wee folk, a faery. She was wild, free, and so full of life. She made us remember what it was to be human. In a way, it *did* make us more human. You see, vampires sometimes find something akin to a true mate."

"A true mate?" It sounded more like a werewolf thing from those movies she'd seen. Then again, she had assumed werewolves and vampires didn't exist. She sure wasn't going to ask about werewolves.

Ian turned to study her over his shoulder. "Vampires aren't like other creatures, we don't have mates like they do, but sometimes we find another who makes us feel alive again. We hunger for the joys of living again, we crave things mortals crave. Our hearts may even beat. We aren't human, but we come close."

"How often do you find these true mates?" she asked, fascinated by the thought of vampires somehow becoming more human.

He shrugged. "Connor and I went a century before we met Lara. She touched us both in that way, and neither of us could resist her."

"You both loved the same woman?" Zoey couldn't imagine that scenario ending well. Both of them struck her as possessive and she'd only known them a short time.

"We did. Lara, bless her, didn't seem to mind. She handled the both of us just fine."

Her face heated and her body flushed with interest. "By both you mean…" she couldn't dare finish.

"In bed. At the same time. We weren't jealous of each other, and she liked us both equally. It was an arrangement all three of us enjoyed." He admitted it so simply, as though he truly hadn't minded it at all.

"Are you and Connor…lovers?" She blushed at her brazen question, but she wanted to know.

Ian shook his head. "No," he chuckled. "Lord, no. We are like brothers. Sharing a woman is something we can do and enjoy doing, if the woman wants both of us."

An image came of her stretched out over Ian's body, him filling her, while Connor was behind her, kissing his way down her back, his hands rubbing…

Zoey shook her head. What a dangerous thought. Tempting too.

"Would you ever do that again? Share a woman with Connor?"

Ian froze, still holding the plates. His face was a painting of sadness, grief coloring his eyes and the shape of sorrow twisting his mouth downward.

"If the right woman came along, another true mate, one who would love us both, perhaps. But I would want to keep her, *forever*. I would want to ask her what I never had the chance to ask Lara. That she turn immortal, so Connor and I wouldn't have to lose her. Neither of us can suffer that again."

Whatever spell of melancholy had woven around his features seemed to ease and vanish. Zoey was thankful. She knew just how deep such wounds could be and how they never fully healed.

She digested his words. Change into a vampire? Could she do something like that? Could she be someone's true mate? The odds were against her, since neither man mentioned she was. It made her heart ache and she rubbed at her chest with one hand.

She waited, ignoring the stab of hunger as best she could, while Ian filled a plate for her. When he returned to the couch, he set two plates of food on the black wooden coffee table.

"So do you drink blood from the vein like Connor, or do you drink from bagged blood or something?" It was a valid question. Connor had after all, sank his teeth into her neck and drank when they'd been…well, no need to dwell on that. Vampires only drank blood in the movies and books, right? Then again, she probably shouldn't be accepting horror movies as any type of truth for what real vampires were capable of.

His lips quirked. "I drink from the vein." Ian lifted her legs up on the couch and sat down, placing her legs onto his lap and settling the thick blanket over them both before reaching for their food.

She took hers gratefully, inhaling the heady scents of the most delicious food she'd ever smelled in her life.

"But you're eating food…" She gestured to the small mountain of tacos he had on his plate, while she picked up a cheeseburger on hers and took a hearty bite. The moan that escaped her lips was very unladylike.

Her mother would have given her a "look" if she'd been there. Her mother had always stressed a woman was judged by her manners. A pang of longing shot through her, momentarily killing the hunger. She'd have given anything to have her mother back, even for just a few minutes.

She sent a silent apology to the heavens.

Sorry, Mom, I'm so hungry.

"Good?" Ian's lips twitched as he took a bite of one of his tacos.

"You have no idea. My last meal was from the garbage can outside that diner where you found me."

"Dear God…"

Shame colored her cheeks. But somehow her ability to filter what she said had gone out the window when she'd started eating. It just felt so good to have something so tasty and warm hitting the empty black hole of her stomach.

She flushed an even deeper red and tried to divert his attention. "So, food. You're a vampire but you can eat it?"

He blinked, eyes softening as he let her change the topic of conversation.

"I can eat. My body doesn't need it, but when I'm inspired, I can certainly enjoy food. I thought it would be rude of me not to eat when you do. It has been several years since I've wanted to eat. I'd forgotten how much I like tacos." He chuckled and offered Zoey a fork.

She took the utensil and used it to fill her mouth with fried rice before replying.

"Inspired?"

"Vampires lose their appetites when they lose interest in life. When you live forever, things around you change faster, even though you do not. When you're a mortal you live life at this breakneck pace, racing to fill up your life with memories, emotions, thoughts and sensations. With a vampire, that's all slowed down to a snail's pace. There's no hurry, no rush. You have forever to do as you wish. And so many things lose their appeal over time."

"What about blood? Do you have to kill someone when you feed?" Her heart pounded harder as she waited for an answer.

"No. It depends, of course, on the vampire. Control is really what matters. Some vampires like to kill, but most do not. The risk of discovery by mortals is too high. Connor and I drink enough to leave the host human healthy. We don't kill." The way he said that last part made her feel as if he almost said "anymore."

"So you really live forever? You don't die or turn all Nosferatu and get all creepy?" she asked.

"No. As long as we have blood every now and then, we stay just the way we are."

"Immortality sounds nice."

Zoey didn't miss the grimace on Ian's face. "It's a curse. When you lose urgency, you find you do very little with your life. It becomes tedious and then meaningless. For men like Connor and me, 'tis hard. We were raised to work, to help others. The idle life of immortality doesn't suit us. We're easily bored. You…however, you fascinate me." His eyes had become bright as Chinese jade. "When I was buying food for you, I had to order some for myself. I wanted to taste the food, see if it was as delicious as I remembered. I was inspired by what you would feel and wanted to experience it myself."

Zoey had a feeling there was some deeper meaning to his words, but she couldn't decipher it, and she was too hungry and tired to give it much thought.

"Oh," she replied. She knew she'd have to face this whole "vampires are real" issue later. After she was full.

His rich baritone laugh made her skin tingle with a new awareness of his masculinity. It intruded upon her instinct to eat. How long had it been since she'd been near a handsome man and been able to think of something other than food and finding a warm place for the night? Too long. Now she was on a stranger's couch, her legs over his lap, sharing a meal in an incredibly intimate setting.

"That's all you have to say? Oh?" He echoed her tone and she laughed. His green eyes lit up again with that light that bewitched her. "You find out we are vampires and you don't have anything else you want to ask?"

Zoey was distracted by the muscles of his throat as he took another bite of a taco. Sure, she had plenty she wanted to ask, but right now she was torn between thoughts of food and sex. A ridiculous giggle bubbled up from her lips. She sounded like a guy. Sex and food on the brain.

"What?" Ian asked, eyeing her thoughtfully.

"Nothing." She resumed eating and with a shrug, so did he.

Once she was stuffed to overflowing, she put the plate on the coffee table and settled deeper into Ian's arms. It was all too much. Her stomach wasn't ready for so much real food after months of near starvation. After only a few minutes, the nausea struck. She struggled out of Ian's grasp and ran for the bathroom.

"Zoey?" Ian's voice was close behind as she reached the toilet and fell to her knees over the porcelain bowl. Her stomach clenched, and she retched violently. Zoey's hands shook on the toilet seat as she coughed and spit up. Cool hands settled on her shoulders, pulled her hair back from her face, keeping it out of the way. Even now, Ian was too good to her.

"Breathe through your mouth, rest your head on your arms," Ian coached. His touch was soothing as he rubbed her back. "I've been to enough late nights at pubs to know how this works."

Her stomach roiled again but she swallowed it down and sucked in a quivering breath.

"I'm so sorry…I ate too much. Should have known."

"It's my fault. I should have remembered you wouldn't be able to handle so much. I would have been better off bringing you soup." His lips brushed her temple in soft kisses.

She winced. "You should leave me…" She coughed again. "I'm not exactly at my best." With a low groan, she spit into the toilet and her stomach twisted again.

His arms wrapped around her and his chin settled on her head. "I'll never leave you, Zoey. Not when you need me the most."

"Why? Why do you care, Ian? I'm nobody to you."

"You're wrong. You mean something to me, love. When I saw you in the alley way, being attacked, I watched you try to protect that book of sketches you have. Against my better judgment, I intervened. When I came over to you, lying there, dying, I saw those sketches and photos all over the ground. You had such vision, you showed such an understanding for life. Someone like that? I couldn't just let them die. And now that I've kissed you," he chuckled, "I think… I might be addicted to your taste." He said the last bit in a teasing tone, but she couldn't help but hope it might be true.

She harrumphed, but managed to smile. "Can I have a glass

of water and some mouthwash? I feel better." It was true. Her body seemed to have relaxed after getting rid of the contents of her stomach. Pity. She'd loved eating all of it and now she had an empty stomach again.

Ian let her go and retrieved what she needed. When she was done rinsing her mouth, she sagged back onto the floor and shut her eyes.

She was so tired. Exhaustion was like a heavy wool blanket, weighing her down and surrounding her with warmth.

"Are you ready to sleep?" Ian's question barely made it through her fatigue.

She nodded jerkily, unable to control herself. She wanted to collapse against him and rely on his strength for support. Again she thought she ought to have been bothered by all this. Why was she so willing to let him take control? But for some reason she trusted him. *An Irish vampire. Imagine that.*

"Up you go." He rose from the bathroom floor, Zoey in his arms. She laid her head on his shoulder, loving how perfect it felt and knowing sadly it wouldn't last. It was her last thought as sleep closed in and swept her away.

CHAPTER FIVE

IAN CARRIED HIS DELICATE BUNDLE down the hall toward his bedroom. He had no intention of taking her anywhere else. She belonged to him, even if she didn't know it yet. Zoey needed someone to look after her and provide for her. It was an old-fashioned notion, perhaps, but he was as old-fashioned as it got. It was a man's duty to spoil his woman and give her everything, even if she didn't need it. Zoey was in desperate need of spoiling.

The rags she'd been wearing—he'd thrown them out as soon as she'd stepped into the shower. He'd peeked of course, seen her enjoying herself and slipped back out, leaving one of his shirts for her to wear. He was a man, not a saint.

Scratch that, he was a vampire, not a man.

He'd been a lusty man even before he'd been turned, as he recalled. The blood lust of a vampire seemed to have heightened his sexual needs and desires. Yet there was a price to it as well. A curse that cut deep.

Because of the glamour, he could never be sure if a woman he was with truly desired him, or was merely responding to *what* he was. It wasn't their fault, they truly believed they felt what they did, only to wake from it like a pleasant dream once he was no longer around.

He just wanted to feel normal, to lust after a woman who truly wanted him back, not worrying about whether it was the vampiric pheromones that lured her into his arms like a docile lamb. When he'd kissed Zoey in the bathroom, it had taken every ounce

of control he had not to lay her on the floor and taste every inch
of her satiny skin. It had been so long since he'd felt that desperate
for a woman in that way.

But she was fragile now. He had to respect her and respect how
she must be feeling. Only a cad like Connor would take advantage of her in such a state.

The damned fool.

"I hope you know what you're doing," Connor muttered from
the doorway.

Speak of the devil and he appears.

"I do."

Ian saw his friend leaning against the doorframe. His arms were
crossed and his brows lowered. Their skittish black cat, Cleo,
rubbed against Connor's ankles, purring loudly. She'd taken a
shine to Connor and vice versa, not that he would ever let Ian see
him return her affections. Ian often heard him talking to the cat
in low soothing tones when he believed Ian couldn't hear.

"What if Seamus comes back, Ian? Do you want another death
on your hands?" Connor's tone seethed with repressed anger.

Ian froze in front of his bedroom door.

Seamus. The name filled him with dread. Life had a funny way
of changing those things that used to seem so certain. Seamus
had once been like a brother to him, just as Connor was, but
when they'd been turned that all changed. Seamus had rejected
the plight of their village, instead choosing to follow in the wake
of their sire, stealing lives and indulging in his thirst for blood.
He'd turned his back on all the things that had made him human.

Ian and Connor had rejected their sire's cruel lust for pain and
death, killing him when they first had the opportunity, and forever making an enemy of their old friend. It had been revenge
that led Seamus to slay their beloved Lara, but Ian knew, as well as
Connor, that the cold fire in Seamus' heart had not dulled since
then. If he found another opportunity to hurt them, he would.

Even knowing that, in his heart Ian was loathe to admit it. "We
haven't seen him since 1923. He won't come back. He took Lara.
Shouldn't he consider himself avenged?"

Connor's bitter laugh was anything but reassuring. "You know better than that. Seamus will never stop. He wants us alone and miserable. It gives him purpose." His eyes burned into Ian's with an intensity born of certainty. "You bring the lass into this, and she's as good as dead. Not tonight or tomorrow, but someday."

Ian looked down at Zoey's face. The dark circles under her long lashes filled him with worry. She needed him. He needed her. He wouldn't let Seamus take her away.

"I'm tired of running away. If he learns of her, if he comes here, I'll be ready. He has no right. If you won't stand up to him, I will." Ian walked away, leaving his friend in the hall without another word.

———•———

A LARGE SILVER-COATED BENGAL CAT LAY stretched out on Ian's bed.

"Off with you, Titus."

Titus was one of their three strays—Cleo, Titus and Lizzy. Cleo rarely left Connor's room and Lizzy was far too independent to stay in either of their rooms. She preferred to make the living room and kitchen her personal space.

Titus raised his head, his golden eyes unwavering as he stood, stretched and pawed the thick bedspread before he finally pounced off the bed and stalked imperiously from the room. Ian grinned. Titus and Connor didn't get along, probably because they had too much in common.

Finally, Ian was alone with Zoey, exactly what he wanted. He set her down on the bed and she stirred. He closed the door and turned back to her. All cleaned up, dressed in one of his shirts, she was an erotic fantasy come to life. A small frame, full of muscles and curves in all the right places, though too thin from lack of food, something he'd soon remedy. Her silky hair tumbled around her face and shoulders in waves.

Soon he hoped to be fisting his fingers through it, tugging as he plundered the sweetness of her mouth. He could tell she was innately passionate. He would work to bring her to climax and savor each little shiver and cry of pleasure as he learned the song of her body. She'd beg for his touch when she was ready, and he'd happily give it to her and more, once she was on fire with arousal.

Ian shrugged out of his clothes and tugged on a pair of flannel pajama pants. He didn't feel the cold, of course, but he wanted Zoey to be warm when she slept next to him, as warm as she could be next to a vampire. He paused, considering this. An electric blanket might not be a bad idea.

He pulled back the thick down comforter and slid his arms under Zoey's back and knees, lifting her up and tucking her into the bed. She sighed, buried her face in the pillow and rolled over as he walked around to the other side.

Her dark lashes fanned up as her eyes opened. Her gaze pierced him like a lance. Such innocence, such life, such hope had once been there, yet it was clouded now by countless days of pain and heartache. To have gone from such happiness to such hopelessness…he knew all too well what that was like.

The night after he turned, the world had become shades of red as he fought his thirst for blood. The vampire who had sired him and Connor, Seamus had cruelly sealed them inside their small cottages with their family members. Unable to escape, he had done the unthinkable and fed on his own parents and his sister, tasting their blood and cursing his soul to hell as he did. Only then, when he lay among their bloodless corpses, did his sire set him free.

Connor had endured the same fate, and there was a hollowness in his friend's gaze that hadn't vanished in two centuries. There had been no tears to shed, but his heart had bled all the same as he'd had to leave his life and his slaughtered family behind. Seamus had fared better, but little did they know it was because he'd found a taste for darkness. They'd had to go with the vampire that sired them, but after a few short years, they'd learned how to survive on their own. Only then did they have the chance to kill their sire and escape, while Seamus swore revenge.

As the decades spun faster and faster past them, he and Conner had grown apart. Connor withdrew into himself and his guilt at living on while his family had died. Until Lara. She had been the key that had brought them back together. A true mate to both of them. He and Connor started enjoying life again, feeling so close to human that it had seemed to be a miracle. Ian's own despair had waned in the burning light of Lara's jubilant life.

But that also ended, as all things must. Seamus had murdered her in cold blood, and they'd been too late to turn her. Her death had forced Ian and Connor apart again. And yet they stuck together. In the end, they had no one else to turn to.

Zoey was still watching him, with eyes that reflected an old soul. A soul that seemed to see right through him.

"Did I fall asleep?" Zoey murmured.

"Only for a few minutes. Go back to sleep."

She blinked, her eyes drifting from his face to his body, over his bare chest and pajamas. He couldn't help it when his body responded and his cock twitched in anticipation. A delicious burn swept across her cheeks, and she pulled the covers up to her chin.

"Are you…are you gonna sleep here too?" There was something so intimate about sleeping next to someone. More intimate than sex. When two bodies occupied a single space, both relaxed and were at their most vulnerable, limbs tangled together, their dreams free to weave together, tying the two people closer than anything else ever could. He knew that for her to sleep next to him would be a sign of trust.

Ian leaned forward, curled his fingers into the comforter's thick white fabric and peeled it away from his side of the bed.

"I'd like to if you don't mind." He made a show of fluffing a pillow and then met her shy gaze with a steady one of his own, hoping it would reassure her.

"Do vampires sleep?"

"When dawn comes we do. It's hard to wake us. We're very groggy if we don't sleep."

"Oh…so it's close to dawn?" Zoey started to sit up, but Ian leaned over her and placed a palm on her shoulder, urging her back down into the bed.

"Dawn is a few minutes away. Is it okay that I sleep here? Next to you?" He wanted her to say yes, to throw her arms around his neck and cover his face with kisses. It was a foolish dream, to want her to genuinely desire him. But it had been so long since he'd known a woman's touch in affection, not because of the influence of his glamour.

Ian waited as she weighed her options. Emotions danced across her expressive face, giving her feelings away in ways she never realized. Her fear, worry, and concern soon turned to desire and eagerness to be with him. He could read every one of her subtle expressions and each fascinated him. It had been many years since a human had captured his interest like this.

"Ian…about what happened in the bathroom, before you went to get the food—"

"I enjoyed it. A lot. If you aren't ready, then you have but to say the word. Just let me sleep here, let me hold you so I know you are safe." There weren't words to tell her how much he needed that.

She'd been so close to death. He'd been lucky enough to bring her back. He was just beginning to realize how fortunate he truly was in saving her. She was a puzzling conundrum of sweetness, independence, creativity and compassion. While she'd showered, he'd taken another look at her art and couldn't wait to ask her a thousand questions about why she chose to sketch and photograph things and people the way she had. Her understanding of the world around her, seeing things others never bothered to look at, fascinated him.

Now that he'd talked with her and kissed her, he couldn't imagine the light of her life being snuffed out like a candle. It would be too much like Lara and he couldn't lose Zoey like that. It was a thought that he knew would haunt him for years, knowing she would someday have to die, as all things did, all except creatures like him and Connor. He just didn't want it to be soon, and not while she was with him.

Vulnerability, fear and need all warred in her soft, sad eyes. Their chocolate depths were filled with heartbreaking memories, weighing him down with a single look. What he wouldn't give to inspire those eyes to spark with life and laughter once again. To turn the sadness he'd glimpsed in her portfolio to pictures and sketches of joy, of beauty.

"Why do you care about me being safe?" Her eyes watered. "No one's cared…not since my family died."

A second later, Ian was in the bed, Zoey's body tucked in his arms as he cradled her against him.

"You need someone to care about you, love. I want to be that person. So let me." He used his fingertips to brush the hair back from her face. Her skin was as soft as the petals of a new flower, like velvet beneath his fingertips. Her pulse beat a rapid rhythm in the delicate blue vein in her neck. Out of pure instinct, his fangs began to lengthen. He struggled to fight off a wave of hunger. She wasn't to be bitten, though Connor had already tasted her. The healed puncture wounds on her neck made his anger flare to life again.

"What's the matter?" she asked, an edge of worry in her tone.

"Connor bit you. I don't like seeing you hurt." He touched the skin where she'd been bitten but she didn't flinch. "I should pound him into a bloody pulp for that."

"It doesn't really hurt. I'd say getting knifed was far worse." She was trying to joke, but it was no doubt a mask to hide the memory of her violent attack.

"You've got to stop saying things that break my heart, lass." Ian pulled her even closer. They were pressed together, skin to skin, from chest to toes and it heated his blood in a way he'd forgotten was even possible.

He rubbed his knuckles over her cheek. Her lashes fluttered and she leaned into him. When she looked up at him, disbelief mixed with exhaustion and humor shone in their depths. They were such a lovely shade of brown—light, almost cinnamon red under the lamp light. He'd never seen a shade of brown so warm and animated before. It fascinated him.

"This is crazy. I'm in bed with a vampire who just wants to cuddle."

"Well, I want more than that, but the last thing I wish to do is force you." He stroked her lower lip with the pad of his thumb.

She glanced up at him. "Every time you touch me, I get this wild urge to kiss you." Her admission made her blush.

With a heavy sigh, he tightened his arms around her. "Zoey, there's something I must tell you about me and Connor. About vampires." He prayed she wouldn't turn away, wouldn't run from him after he'd explained things.

"Okay." She dragged the word out, as though attempting to calm herself, but he didn't miss her increased heartbeat.

"Vampires have a magnetic pull to them. Most of us call it a glamour, because with prolonged exposure, a mortal will begin to see things fuzzily, so strong is the desire to be with us. Like clouding your senses. It helps to lure prey to us and make them aroused. Willing. 'Tis hard to tell what's true desire and what is from this pull."

"A magnetic pull?" Zoey asked, brows drawn together as she seemed to puzzle her way through the information.

"Yes. We used to consider it magic, but I think perhaps it is more compared to animal pheromones. It acts on a mortal sub-consciously, but powerfully."

"Vampire mojo," she whispered to herself. "I was right."

"Vampire mojo?" Ian almost laughed, but sobered when she answered him with a grave nod.

"I couldn't figure out why I was terrified of Connor chasing me, but the second he was close to me, I just wanted him too much to care about how frightened I was."

Ian stroked a hand along one of her arms, seeking to soothe her. "That's why I was furious with Connor. He took advantage of you, knowing how you would react."

She shook her head. "No, he didn't. I remember him asking me if that's what I wanted, and there was this moment of clarity, like that crazy desire had been lifted, but I still wanted him. Just like I still want you," she added the last in a shy little whisper.

"You want me?" He was too afraid to hope it was true. But how was he to know? Too many years had been wasted in his early years after turning, as he'd tried to figure out whether a mortal woman was truly interested in him, or whether it was the work of the glamour. Aside from Lara, it had always been the glamour, and that realization had always been painful.

"I do, but I'm so afraid that you don't want me back, that it's just my appeal as a walking Happy Meal that draws you in." Her words would have made him laugh, but the fear of rejection in her lovely eyes cut him soul deep.

"You are irresistible, Zoey. If I didn't hear that sweet little heartbeat thumping so madly against my chest, I'd have to question whether or not you might be the one with a glamour."

Her skeptical little scoff had him grin as she wrinkled her nose. "I doubt I'm irresistible."

"You know…a man might call that a challenge." He couldn't help but stare at her lips, drawn to the movement of her tongue slipping out to wet her lips. What would it feel like to have that tongue lick him, or those lips wrap around his cock as she sucked him into oblivion? She would be a natural, with her sensual curiosity. A devious, but shy smile danced across her lips. She was new to this sort of teasing, but he sensed she was enjoying it. She was challenging him, but not outright.

"A man? But not a vampire?" she asked.

Ian's lip's tilted up into a smile. She was brave enough after all.

"Be warned, Zoey. You challenged me." He curled one arm around the back of her neck, pillowing her head as he rolled on top of her. Her knees were locked together, but when he lowered his head and stole her lips, she softened. A few more seconds at the opening of her mouth, and once he'd gained entrance, her legs fell apart. He slid his hips between her knees and groaned as he settled into the cradle of her thighs.

It had been years since he'd allowed himself to truly enjoy a woman's body like this. She was built perfectly, small, compact. He loved spanning his hands over a woman's full thighs as he licked at her center, and he would do this with Zoey before long. Yes, he would thoroughly taste her in every way possible.

He coaxed her lips farther apart to slide his tongue inside. Her startled gasp made it impossible to resist deepening the kiss further. He wanted inside her mouth, inside her. He desired her, wanted to possess every part of her, even her heart…as foolish and dangerous as that was.

Zoey's hands explored his back, shaping the contour of Ian's muscles. He purred like a tiger at her eager touch. She tilted her head back, exposing her throat. He could hear the excited clatter of her heartbeat. He nuzzled her neck, then licked the spot where her pulse beat against her skin, the place where Connor left puncture wounds. The faint taste of dried blood was still there, calling to him like a siren's song. The urge was too hard to fight. He rubbed his hips against hers, grinding against the heated core of her body which was now blissfully bare to him since the shirt had ridden high on her waist.

Ian dropped his head and gripped her neck with his teeth, letting his fangs hold her still. He didn't break the skin, but his need to bite, to mark his prey was overwhelming…

Prey!

No. Zoey wasn't prey. She was his charge. She needed his protection. Ian let his fangs recede as he stared down at her. Her eyes were glazed over with desire. Her lips were swollen from his kisses and all he wished to do was to keep nibbling them like succulent fruit.

"Do you believe me now, Zoey? My sanity is practically in shreds." He pressed his hard shaft against her, both thankful for the shield of his pajamas and disappointed he couldn't slide against her slick sex and feel it against his cock.

The temptation would be too great. He'd sink into her, take the innocence he knew was there and not give her the proper love-making she deserved for their first time together. Sure, she was acting well enough as though she knew what to do, but he knew a sensual innocent when he saw one. Despite his body's needs, it was too soon. She deserved to be seduced, courted, wooed. He would give that to her, even if it killed him. They both deserved to know what lay between them wasn't the result of the glamour, but from true desire. His heart gave another strange little tug and he winced, breathing almost painfully for an instant.

"Why'd you stop?" Her hands rested on his shoulders, her fingertips caressed his neck.

"Because you're tired and need to rest, and I won't be able to stay awake much longer."

Zoey's lips formed the most adorable pout. "But I don't want to stop."

"I know, love, I know. But you're exhausted. There's plenty of time later." He kissed the tip of her nose. "Go to sleep."

She scowled. "No." Her brows drew down in a line and her lips plumped in a deeper pout than before.

He narrowed his eyes and focused, using his power of influence. "Go to sleep, Zoey."

She continued to scowl, but it was lessened by a heavy yawn. Her lashes batted up and down wearily.

"Did you just vampire voodoo me? I'm…" Another yawn broke her words apart. "Can't keep…my…" Her lashes fell and stayed fanned out over her cheeks. Her breathing slowed, as did her heartbeat. Her hands dropped from his neck to her sides.

Ian's body screamed in frustration. He focused on maudlin thoughts of the years when he and Connor had been mortal. It stilled his body's needs and brought him down from the blissful high of kissing Zoey. Kissing her was like looking up at the night sky, seeing endless stars or submerging himself in the ocean, feeling the waves roll past his body. It was powerful, unending, bigger than any one person.

With just one simple brush of his lips on hers, he no longer felt like Ian Kennedy. He wasn't an immortal, wasn't a man, he felt like something more, something greater. It made him want something, something he'd dared not hope for since he'd been turned. He dared not breathe the word. He wasn't ready and neither was she.

Instead he focused on Zoey and her power over him. The way she overwhelmed his senses. He'd never been that aroused, that lost in the moment with any other woman, except with Lara. He forced his mind away from those memories. She was many years gone and Zoey was here. Sweet, vibrant Zoey. It was time to start over, to live his life again. Seamus and Connor be damned. He was going to enjoy this Christmas.

CHAPTER SIX

CONNOR O'SHEA LAY ON HIS back in bed, glowering at the ceiling. One palm rested on his stomach, the other behind his head, providing a cushion. He was mad enough to punch something, but he wasn't that sort of man. He never let his temper manifest in anything but his words.

His father had used his fists, and Connor swore he'd never be like that. When a woman got his ire up, he tended to seduce, and then fuck her into blissful submission. Zoey wasn't like other women. It wasn't just her body that held him fascinated. It was the way her emotions flitted across her face, so full of expression, of meaning. After nearly two centuries mortals had become faceless, nameless, a means to an end for him. A way to survive. But not so with Zoey. He'd tasted her blood and what he'd seen through the connection, one he hadn't meant to allow, would have knocked him flat if he hadn't been on the bed.

A vampire could connect to their prey while feeding, but as a vampire grew more disciplined they could shut out the connection. He had been too lost in his game of capture and claiming of Zoey that he hadn't been prepared to block out her memories.

They'd rushed through him in wild, brilliant flashes, like summer lightning striking in the distance. *Warmth of a noon day sun upon his skin, the sound of wind chimes tinkling in a faint breeze, the excitement of blowing out birthday candles, a room heavy with the scent of sugar and melting wax.*

A hundred days of light and laughter had embedded themselves into his soul. She'd given him a gift of her life and she'd never known it. A mortal life with mortal blessings. One he could take into the darkness of his own heart. His chest squeezed and he huffed, suddenly short of breath. What a strange sensation. He hadn't ever done that before…except once, long ago with Lara. That had been a time when his body had seemed to revert back to its most human state, *almost* human at any rate. Did that mean…?

No, Lara was my true mate. And Lara is gone. This is fascination, nothing more. An echo of what I lost.

He didn't know what to do about Zoey. She was fiery, passionate, yet she seemed too sweet. He preferred his women wicked, wanton, willing to try anything in bed or out. He doubted Zoey would ever be so bold…

Yet her eyes had darkened with such fire when he'd brought her to climax. Her sheath had been tight, wet and so hot it scorched his fingers. She wasn't a virgin, no, but she was damned close. The right man, or former man, could tempt her to release the wanton woman he'd seen in those eyes.

He'd known right away she hadn't been with a man in quite some time. The look of shock on her face when she'd come—like she'd never felt such a violent outburst of pleasure before—nearly undid him. It would have been heaven to sink into her wet center and feel her walls clench down around him. He'd have taken her slow at first, built up to a blinding, pounding rhythm and have her screaming for more, harder and harder until they both collapsed in exhaustion from ecstasy.

Connor snarled and leapt out of bed. "Fuck!" He stalked out into the hall and into the bathroom. He stepped into the shower and cranked the knob over to cold, praying it would shock him out of his state of need.

The water helped a little, but he was still too aroused over the helpless, little, human female. He needed to stop thinking about her, about the way she felt beneath him, the scent of her skin mixed with the natural scent of her desire. His own skin seemed to glow with a hint of color, a faint hum of warmth despite the icy water sluicing over his skin. Yet another sign of a true mate.

Bloody hell.

Connor shut off the water and stormed out of the shower, frustrated that he couldn't make his body forget her. He curled a towel around his hips, scowling at the tent that popped up. He stopped in the hall, arrested by the most intriguing aroma. He couldn't remember the last time he'd smelled something that good.

Curious, he padded toward the kitchen, following the scent like a bloodhound. It led to the take-out bags left on the counter. He opened the nearest sack and peered inside. Several small items were wrapped with wax paper. He reached in and retrieved a… taco? He unwrapped it and lifted it to his nose. The spices and the meat smelled good. *Really good.* He'd walked by a taco food truck just the other day and yet the scent there had been dull, a fraction of what he was taking in now. Connor cocked one hip against the bar and then took a huge bite. The taste exploded in his mouth, his taste buds set alive by the rich flavors.

He scarfed down the rest of the tacos and explored the other sacks with growing interest, his stomach still rumbling.

After fifteen minutes he'd downed half the fried rice, cheeseburgers and spaghetti, washing all of this down with three colas. His stomach was fit to burst, but the fullness was fantastic. It had been ages since he'd felt such need or felt so satisfied. How long had it been since he'd eaten human food? It had to have been before the Second World War…right after Lara died.

Connor eyed the empty take-out bags.

The sound of murmurs and sighs from Ian's room reached him. With a sinking feeling, he was facing the simple truth again.

Zoey. It had to be. She'd resurrected his appetite and, from the sounds of it, Ian's sex drive. Connor's as well, as much as he hated to admit it. He'd been as randy as a stoat when he'd gotten her on her back earlier. A frown tugged at his lips. He didn't want this. He didn't want to be reminded of everything he'd lost. Everything they'd both lost. And what they could lose again.

No more true mates, no more mortal lovers. I'm done with them.

Damn that Zoey Blake and her petal soft lips and killer curves. She was going to be the death of both of them.

Ian's room grew quiet. No more sweet murmurs or little sounds of lovemaking. Zoey's light breathing penetrated the silence, but that was all. Connor glanced about the kitchen and the living room, feeling oddly alone. He'd never minded before now how barren their house was, or how not having a woman of his own felt. But now it did. There were no photos except the ones Ian took of places they'd lived, nor items from the old days to remind either him or Ian of the passing years. They'd both thought it best to keep looking forward.

He and Ian had lived here for three years, and in that time they'd never met the neighbors or even spent time making this place a home. They couldn't afford to, not when they had to move every fifteen years so people wouldn't notice they didn't age. Immortality was a stagnant state of existence, yet they were always moving, leaving life after life behind. Zoey's presence in the house added something that he'd sorely missed, and it scared the hell out of him. Life was always followed by death, and he was so bloody tired of death, except, perhaps, his own.

Connor threw out the empty take-out bags. Lizzy bumped against his shin, purring, and he bent down to stroke her. He'd given Ian hell for bringing the cats home at first, but he'd soon learned to tolerate having the animals around. Perhaps he even enjoyed them. It put him into a routine, feeding and caring for them. Although he'd never tell Ian, it was nice to have something alive to touch every now and then. Something that wouldn't end up being his dinner, that is.

He would have preferred to seduce a woman and stroke her instead of a cat, but women were too much trouble, and he'd long since abandoned pursuing them. The only females who received his undivided attention now were Lizzy and Cleo. Titus, the male cat, avoided him and the feeling of distrust was mutual.

The cats were good for Ian too. They seemed to ground him. Give him purpose. Connor hated that he and Ian hadn't spent much time together in the last twenty years and it was putting a strain on their relationship. Even though they lived under the same roof, he and Ian took turns going out to hunt for their meals, avoiding each other as much as possible. It hadn't been on purpose, but now he saw that they'd fallen into a comfortable pattern living as near strangers. They'd once been like brothers, but the years had distanced them and he longed to get that brotherly camaraderie back.

Once again his mind strayed back to Zoey. No doubt she'd be a strain on their relationship too. Ian would want to keep her, like every stray he came across. And Connor would protest. But Zoey was human, not a cat. If she stayed, he'd end up bedding her. It was only natural; she was an attractive woman and he had only the wickedest thoughts of what he'd like to do to her. He was man enough to admit it. If Zoey stayed under his roof, he'd have her on her back, screaming in pleasure before long.

But Ian wanted her too…hence the complication.

They'd been able to share Lara with no jealousy. She'd loved them both and they'd cared only for her happiness. They had feared it would be hard to be with a woman and share her since neither man was attracted to the other, but she had made it easy. She'd been one of a kind.

Connor doubted Zoey would be willing to share a bed with two men, even if their sole intent was to fuck her mindless with pleasure.

A wave of sudden fatigue rushed through his limbs, and Connor knew he'd delayed too long in getting back to his room. Dawn must be minutes away. The exhaustion was numbing. Fighting it off, he stripped his towel and dropped it halfway down the hall. He stumbled into his room just as the heavy metal blinds installed in his windows dropped down, settling him in darkness. Though the daylight would not kill him, it would put him into a heavy sleep and if left too long, it would eventually burn his skin severely. He collapsed onto his bed, letting exhaustion chase him into darkness.

Damn, he wanted to be holding the mysterious sensual Zoey. But she was with Ian…

*T*HE THIN LAYER OF ICE *on the black asphalt was more treacherous than Zoey realized, until it was too late. She tightened her
mitten-covered hands over the steering wheel but her grasp slipped. Tires
squealed and the light from her headlights spun out over the cliff's edge.*

*Zoey screamed, but it was cut short as the car skidded past the end of
the thin metal railing. There was one moment where the world seemed
frozen, and then it all dropped away. The pit of her stomach collapsed and
seconds later, the screech of metal and the horrible crashing of her world
began.*

*The car rolled over and over. Snow, ice and rocks exploded through the
empty space where the windshield had shattered. When the car came to
a final stop, Zoey was trapped, her seat belt strangling the life out of her.
She couldn't breathe. Her mittens dug into the belt but she couldn't get
hold of it to jerk it off. Black dots spotted her vision and white pain seared
her body. Even hanging upside down, the vision in her cracked rear view
mirror was all too clear.*

*Her parents were in the back seat. Blood across their faces, their eyes
wide and sightless as they looked out past her, seeing only what the dead
could see.*

"No…please, God, no…"

Zoey woke with a desperate wail of deepest agony. Cold tears
dried down her cheeks and wet the pillow below her. Cold arms
were wrapped around her body and she felt the shape of a masculine body curled up behind her. For a moment she couldn't
remember where she was or who she was with. The icy cold
body startled her, as though she'd woken up with a corpse, and
she frantically scrambled out of bed. The body in the sheets didn't
move and she could barely make out the man's features in the
near pitch darkness.

The awful memory of that horrible night was submerged
beneath the tide of memories from the last several hours—the
sharp sting of the stabbing in the alley, the surprise of Ian's sudden
rescue, the burn of his kiss, the ache of her body beneath Connor's. Ian. It was Ian in the bed. Her heart started to beat again
at a frantic pace, as though desperate to catch up with itself after
being still for several seconds.

Ian's bedroom was so dark that Zoey was hesitant to move at first. She didn't want to stub her toe on a bedpost. Her eyes sought the only source of light, a sliver of gold that crept in from beneath the door to the hallway. She tugged the edge of Ian's shirt down and shivered. It would be so easy to crawl back into bed with him, but he was so cold. His heart didn't beat. It was not the most comforting or natural thing when she started to think about it.

Zoey didn't want to go back to sleep, not just yet. The dream still lurked in the corners of her mind. The guilt that ate away at her threatened to resurface. Her mouth was dry. A glass of water would be good. There had been too many nights where she hadn't slept well due to dehydration. She eased the door open and slipped into the hall, looking for the kitchen.

The clock on the sleek black oven read 3:45 PM. She'd slept through most of the day? It was such a relief to realize she'd gotten more than a few hours of sleep in one sitting.

After finishing two glasses of water, she set it in the dishwasher. Everything in the cupboards was brand new and seemed to be unused. Zoey wondered if Ian and Connor even owned dishwashing detergent. Probably not.

"Couldn't sleep?"

The husky murmur behind her ear was so soft and unexpected that she let out a squeak of surprise.

She turned and came face to face with Connor's bare chest. He was so tall she had to tip her head back to look him in the eye. She swallowed hard. His face was inscrutable, but the curve of his mouth had distracted her from whatever she'd been about to say. Warm brown eyes, like hot cocoa.

His answering laugh shook her as he pressed close. Something hard dug into her stomach and she jolted in shock.

"Easy, pet. 'Tis just my body making its desires known." He curled one hand around the back of her neck, possessive and dominating yet not harmful. The message was clear. She wasn't to move, to escape until he allowed it.

"You're naked!" Her voice was too shrill and breathless as she took in in the length of his lean, muscled…gloriously bare body.

The blush that burst on her cheeks was hot enough that she broke out into a sweat. Rope after rope of corded muscle formed a six-pack of abs; she could feel every smooth hard contour as her breasts pressed against it. Damn, he was too tall, how could they ever…

Zoey shook her head, failing to clear the fog of lust that swamped her. Never in her life had she been so close to losing all sense of control. This had to be what Ian told her about, the glamour, the vampire mojo as she liked to call it. There didn't seem to be a world outside those perfect pectorals and biceps. There was just him. Connor. One hundred percent male. And she was a tiny delicate female by comparison. Knowing that he desired her sent bursts of electricity through her, both weakening her body and strengthening her own desires.

Connor's fingertips stroked her throat, the cool press of his fingers a balm to her fiery, sweat-covered skin. His gaze seemed slumberous as he looked down at her. She was a goner. He'd have his teeth in her neck, and she didn't stand a chance.

"Shall we get you naked too?" The suggestion flowed from his sensual lips with such lazy confidence that Zoey's knees turned to jelly. She would have collapsed onto the floor at his feet, but she stayed upright because his hips jerked forward, digging into hers, keeping her pinned.

"What do you think? Lose the shirt and show me that pretty skin, Zoey…" Her name, so often sounding childish when anyone else said it, sounded positively erotic the way the syllables rolled off his tongue. Her head felt light as she sucked in a harsh, much needed breath.

"Umm…" Nope, there would be no more articulate words from her today. *Cavewoman meet Caveman*, her inner voice giggled wildly.

Her mind blanked as he cupped her ass and lifted her into the air, then set her down onto the counter, bringing her face level to his. His hands cupped her cheeks, keeping her still. There was the barest hint of hesitation in his eyes, and then he took her mouth hard. She had no choice but to open up as he thrust his tongue inside. He seemed determined to devour her, consume her with his frantic play. Her hands found their way to his shoulders, digging her nails into him.

Connor's hands molded around her shoulders, squeezed, then slid down inch by inch along her back, tracing the curve of her spine until he found her hips and tugged hard, dragging her to the edge of the counter. His cock rubbed against her open folds, and she whimpered at the violent need she felt to have him inside her. He rocked, teasing mercilessly, but never giving her what her body screamed for.

"Oh, God, please!" she rasped between deep, drugging kisses.

His hands kneaded her ass, the movement along with his gyrating hips was going to end her… He seemed to sense that she was fraying at the edges and drew his head back, gazing directly at her. His eyes, once brown, were almost black now and wreathed with just a hint of crimson around the pupil that would have scared her if she hadn't been driven insane with sexual need.

His hands moved back up to her shirt at the collar and in one swift move, tore the shirt apart. Buttons went flying as he tossed the clothing away. He growled low as he held her away from him to stare at her exposed breasts. They felt swollen and heavy, the tips peaked and begging for his attention. She was too shy to ask, so she arched her back, offering them to him without words. Conner dropped his head to her neck, nibbling her collarbone with frustrating tenderness, then moving lower.

Zoey hissed as he took the nipple in his mouth. He suckled hard, pulling on the tip, his tongue laving and his teeth scraping over it until she whimpered and moaned. Waves of heat assailed her and she fisted her hands in his dark blond hair. Her eyes clamped shut as cold air teased her breasts. He lifted his mouth away and straightened.

He grabbed her by the waist and carried her over to the couch in the living room, stretching her out beneath him. Before she could react he'd flipped her onto her stomach and covered her body with his. She felt his cock slide between the cleft of her ass as he slid against her from above. His mouth was on her neck, kissing, licking, nibbling. One forearm rested by her shoulder, propping him up enough to prevent him from crushing her. His other hand cupped her breast, squeezed, pinched her nipple and smoothed its way down her waist to the fiery wet heat between her thighs.

She raised her hips up, encouraging him to enter from behind, to take what she freely offered. His next growl sent skittering tingles along her spine as he cupped her between her legs, pressing the heel of his palm on her clit. She pushed against his hand, trying to rub against him, anything to satisfy the need clawing at the insides of her body.

She cried out Connor's name as he slid his thigh between hers, pressing against her bottom, the added pressure sending her over the cliff of self-control. She turned her head over her shoulder, needing his mouth on hers. He complied, briefly dueling with her tongue, feeding her thirst for more of everything, more of him.

"I need…need…" Before she could get out the rest he sunk three fingers deep into her, pushing her open, stretching her to accommodate him. This was beyond anything she'd ever dreamed of, all muscle and strength, passion and sex in one tall, exciting package. He'd fuck her into a coma if she let him, and she wanted to let him. Sleeping with Connor would strip her of her soul. She'd become a mindless wanton creature craving him and only him and the idea was *so* appealing.

Connor didn't waste time as he worked her body to a frenzied climax. He rocked himself against her bottom, mimicking the harried patterns of a wild mating.

Her head flew back, pressing against his shoulder as she came. He continued to work his fingers, refusing to give her time to breathe as he brought ripple after ripple of ecstasy to the surface. Her body quaked, her limbs spasming beneath his body.

Something warm splashed on her lower back and Connor shouted a curse, muffling it somewhat by lightly sinking his teeth into her shoulder, enough so that the sting sent a second smaller orgasm through her already weakened and sated body. The only thing that stung her in that moment was knowing he hadn't been inside her. Was he concerned about pregnancy? Was that even possible with vampires?

Finally, he released her neck, kissing the bruised skin before he sighed and rested his cheek against her.

Connor held her for a long moment, neither of them thinking or speaking, just his body above hers, keeping her pinned to the couch as they both recovered. She didn't want to move, couldn't move. She wanted to stay here forever. Nothing else had to exist outside this moment. One wondrous moment followed by soft breathing and the gentle journey of coming down from heights of pleasure.

The haze of desire was gone, but in its place was something more, something concrete she could cling to. Not glamour. Whatever had just happened between them, and what she was feeling now, that wasn't because of that. Her thoughts were lucid now, even as tired as she was, and she *still* wanted him, wanted to be in his arms, even just to be held.

Zoey's eyes had almost drifted closed when she felt Connor shift above her and get up. She protested with a lazy "No…"

He returned with a damp dishtowel. Smoothing the towel over her lower back and between her thighs, he wiped her clean. She ought to have been embarrassed, but she was too exhausted to care. He got up again, disappeared through a door just off the kitchen, probably the laundry room. Turning on her side, she watched him as he walked back. He was so beautiful and…still aroused. She dropped her eyes and blushed, all too aware of him and his… She shut her eyes and feigned a yawn.

A cool breeze drifted over her skin and with it she returned to some semblance of reality. She was lying naked on a couch in a house with two men she barely knew, and she'd had sex…well… sort of…with one of them. And she couldn't forget the most ridiculous part of it. They were *vampires*. That part never seemed to get less strange, and yet she questioned so little about it.

"You should go back to Ian's room, lass," Connor said. His voice forced her to look at him again. He was standing there, arms crossed, still completely naked, watching her.

Zoey rubbed her eyelids. Maybe this was all some strange dream. Maybe she was still dying in that alley and this was all some hallucination as her body shut down. The thought made her shiver and not in a good way. But this couldn't be a dream because everything felt too real.

Maybe I should just accept this for what it is. Any woman would kill to be in her place right now with two gorgeous men…er… vampires, interested in her.

It was the second time she'd given in to Connor's seduction. Shame should have weighed her down, but instead there was only a melancholy fatigue. She forced herself to get up and retrieve the torn white shirt from the kitchen floor. She slipped her arms into the oversized sleeves and tugged it back over her body, thankful for even the minimal cover it provided. The buttons were gone, but the shirt was large enough to wrap around her like a robe. Connor stayed still, studying her with his honey-brown eyes, no longer black and the pupils not wreathed with fire anymore. Human eyes. Not the eyes of a predator.

Under the weight of Connor's stare, she dared not raise her own eyes. She fled down the hall back to the sanctuary of Ian's room. She slid back into his arms, glancing at the glowing red numbers of the clock on the nightstand. It was already after four in the afternoon. She'd slept most of the day away, which didn't really matter, given that she was now apparently on a vampire time schedule.

In a few more hours Ian would probably be awake. Why had Connor been up? Was he less affected by the sun than Ian? She'd have to ask one of them later. She was curious enough to risk that. She pulled the thick down comforter higher up on her and the movement woke Ian. He shifted, tightened his hold around her waist, brushed his lips over her cheek in a sweet sleepy kiss and then dozed off again.

Guilt filled her with an extra helping of self-loathing. Twice now she'd been pleasured by one man and run straight into the arms of another… God, was she that easy? There wasn't another way to see it. She despised herself, lusting after two men. One who clearly intended to use her, and one who clearly wanted a relationship. She kept giving herself over to the wrong man. It should have been Ian, the man who'd professed to care about her, that she should have been with. Shouldn't it?

What had happened to make her this way? Was it losing her parents, or was it when her life had crumbled around her and she'd realized she would do anything for food and a warm place to sleep? She'd never sold herself. She'd escaped that fate…so far. Was staying with Ian and Connor the same thing? Did it matter that she hungered for them and the passion their touch inspired in her?

Ian shifted next to her, nuzzled her neck and grazed his teeth along the sensitive skin leading up to her ear. She sighed and stirred restlessly as tingles of fresh arousal burst inside her like a flash-bang. Her body should have been too tired to respond with any interest, but here she was, hungering for Ian.

"You okay?" Ian murmured.

She rolled over to face him, curling into him as he pulled the blankets up to her chin.

"I got thirsty." The half lie fell bitter on her lips.

Ian's nose touched hers, rubbing in an Eskimo kiss that had her blush. She melted when he put his lips to hers. The kiss was fire and honey combined. The need for more was there, but he controlled it, even though he settled a hand on the flare of her hips, pushing the white shirt up past her stomach. The sensation of him being naked there, his hand so close to the apex of her thighs had her quivering all over again. He dug his fingers into her with the barest hint of a bite and she arched into him, capturing his lips as her own need made her lose her grip on her control.

When she broke the kiss, he gave a smile that made his eyes crinkle. "I was thinking, when we get up later, we could go Christmas tree shopping. Connor and I don't have one but since you're here it would be nice to do things properly. You'll stay here with us for Christmas, won't you? I know you want to get back on your feet, but jobs will be scarce until after the holidays."

Zoey's fingertips traced the strong line of his jaw as she considered his offer. She wanted to stay, but should she?

"Do vampires celebrate Christmas?"

"Connor and I do. We're Catholics and haven't been struck by lightning entering a church yet, so I've got to believe we're not creatures of evil. Connor threw a vial of holy water at me once, claimed it was for test purposes, but I knew he was in a foul mood that day. Nothing happened of course. Just got wet." He chuckled.

Zoey pondered that. She hadn't even considered that Ian or Connor might be evil. She knew they were vampires, but neither of them had made her skin crawl like the man who'd attacked her in the alley, who had been all too human. Perhaps vampirism wasn't religious but scientific, like their bodies evolved, or were affected by a virus in the blood of another vampire, rather than anything supernatural. Theories about vampires in popular culture seemed to welcome every possible explanation these days. She wished she knew what the truth was, but it seemed even Ian and Connor didn't know what they really were.

Turning back to their conversation, and Christmas, she grinned hopefully up at him.

"You'd really buy a tree just for me?"

His lips curved in a boyish smile. "Absolutely. Wouldn't be Christmas without one."

"Okay. I'll stay."

"Good. I would hate to have to vampire voodoo you into staying," he teased.

She punched his chest. "No more of that, thank you very much."

"Very well," he sighed. "Go back to sleep, I'll wake you in a few hours when it's evening."

Content enough to agree, she tucked her head under his chin and snuggled closer. His skin was cold, but it warmed where she touched him and falling asleep was all too easy.

She prayed the nightmare wouldn't return.

CHAPTER SEVEN

CONNOR LEANED AGAINST THE KITCHEN counter, palms spread on the granite. He was still naked and aroused as hell. The residual guilt he normally felt when finding any level of satisfaction since Lara's death hadn't surfaced. Another sort of guilt did. He'd just taken Zoey—or rather, *almost* taken her—seduced her with her own desire as he'd done to countless others. She'd enjoyed it, of course, but that didn't mean what he'd done had been right, regardless of why he'd done it.

It was the dream. He'd been unable to stand looking into her eyes and seeing the remnants of the nightmare that had woken her up. He'd been there with her through every silent scream, every panicked second of the night that had changed her life.

He hadn't meant to get inside her head. Ian had the power to influence and manipulate mortals, but Connor's immortal gift was different. One minute Connor had been lost in the darkness of his own dreams, and the next he was caught up in Zoey's mind. Invisible, yet experiencing her fear as she lost control of the car and went over the cliff's edge. He'd felt the impact that had killed her parents, yet she'd somehow survived. He wasn't sure how she'd escaped the car; she'd jerked awake before he could see the rest. He'd woken as well, body shaking as though he'd been hit with a shot of adrenaline.

It had taken every ounce of his self-control not to march into Ian's room and steal the scared little woman away and offer her the comfort she needed. But he'd waited, listening to the padding of her bare feet on the kitchen floor and the creak of the faucet as she got a glass of water. But soon he couldn't resist any longer.

When he ventured into the hall and saw her in the shirt and nothing else, rational thought fled and his libido had taken over. He had to touch her, taste her, tease her, please her. Anything to erase the wounded shadows in her eyes.

He hadn't intended to sate himself as well, but she'd been so deliciously wild in her release that he'd come all over her delectably round backside. It had shamed him as much as it had embarrassed her. He'd cleaned her as best he could, but she'd still turned tail and ran from him. Straight back to Ian.

He cursed and pounded a fist against the granite counter. The stone cracked. There was no going back to sleep, not while he was on edge like this. He was able to shrug off the daylight easier than Ian and had little trouble staying awake when he had to. In an hour the sun would be low in the sky. He needed to get out, breathe the fresh air, restore his sanity.

Connor went back to his room, pulled his clothes on and stepped back into the hall. There were soft murmurs in Ian's room again. Talk of Christmas trees…

Conner snarled silently. Well, there was only one way he could think of to compete with Ian and his damned romantic side. He could offer Zoey things she needed, practical things, not just trees and nostalgia. A woman needed clothes to stay warm in this weather. And if it so happened that he was able to help her in and out of those clothes…well, he'd show her just what else he could offer once she was flat on her back beneath him.

Connor returned to the kitchen, found his wallet and keys and left the house. His Land Rover was parked in the driveway, a light bit of snow dusting the windows and car roof. The evening sun drooped over the treetops to the west. Lethargy struggled to take hold of him, but he'd always been strong. With enough rest, he could resist its call. It was a pity that a strong cup of coffee wouldn't help, though. His vampiric metabolism didn't allow caffeine or alcohol to affect his body.

Christmas lights adorned the rooftops and lined the sidewalks.

Only their house lacked any such merry twinkle. He'd never bothered with lights before, but now he wished he'd had. Perhaps he should.

Connor shook his head and headed for his car. He brushed the snow off the windows and got inside. There was a mall nearby and he could get what he needed there.

The sun's fading UV rays didn't penetrate his Land Rover's tinted windows, and the rush of energy that came from the darkness of his car was a relief. Connor had learned to love the heavy cloak of darkness and the power that came with it. Zoey was like the night, a clear midnight with a bright moon. She enveloped him, energized him, made his every dark desire writhe in the shadows of his heart. She made him long for tangled sheets and sweat-soaked limbs twining in the erotic movements of wild sex.

The images had his body rioting with arousal once again. No. Zoey needed sweetness and soft wooing, the sort of things Ian would give her.

Connor navigated the streets, driving carefully, never more aware of the danger of ice-slickened roads. He couldn't erase Zoey's memory of her car shooting off the edge and crashing in the snow.

Holiday shoppers packed the sidewalks when Connor reached the mall. Parking was hell, but Connor waited until a spot opened. Patience was just one of the few perks of being immortal. A mother passed by his car as he pulled into a spot, towing her three children in a line. They toddled after her in marshmallow-shaped winter coats sporting a rainbow of bright colors. The last little boy, who looked to be about four years old, stopped and stared at Connor from beneath a ski cap and scarf up to his nose. Connor shut his car door, locked it and slid the keys into his pocket, watching the boy with the same interest.

The boy tilted his head back to stare up at Connor.

"Are you a giant?" the boy asked in the way children always did when they noticed something obvious that no adult would ever consider saying out loud.

"I am, and you're quite the wee lad, aren't you?" he replied.

He'd had plenty of siblings when he'd been alive and knew to answer a child with an answer akin to what they'd asked. It made them feel more grown up, which was quite important to children.

"Yup!" The boy agreed. "Merry Christmas, Mister!" His muffled exclamation had Connor's lips tug up in a reluctant smile.

"And to you," he echoed. He didn't like to think about his own family, the one he'd had to kill when the need for blood had taken over and he'd been locked inside the house with them. They'd been starving, on the verge of death, but it hadn't mattered. Both he and Ian had murdered their own kin because they hadn't known how to control their bloodlust. But that was the past, a very distant one. He focused on the happy memories, the ones that made him smile—it was that or feel his heart bleed again and again for the rest of his eternal life.

He turned to face the monstrous mall and squared his shoulders. If mothers with children could survive the frenzy, he could as well. Surely it couldn't be as bad as the wars he'd fought in over the last two centuries.

The throngs of people would surely have suffocated him, if he'd needed to breathe. Thankfully he did not. His body still drew breath, out of habit more than anything, but it was unnecessary. Long ago he'd been dumped in Dublin Bay with iron boots on because of a bad debt—it had taken him two days to walk back to shore to find a blacksmith to remove them.

The first stop he made was a department store. A nice-looking woman in her mid-thirties, wearing a nametag that read "Candace" smiled knowingly as he took in the endless clothes racks.

"Overwhelming, isn't it?" Her eyes were warm and her smile genuine.

"A bit." His voice dropped low as he made sure no one else could hear him admit it.

"Who are you shopping for? I can help," Candace offered, a bright smile warning him that he ought to control his effect on her before she gave him her phone number. Connor was ready to refuse but then realized he did need help. He willed himself to be less desirable. It was strange to think that a physical affect like the glamour could be controlled through his will alone, but that was how it worked.

"It's my woman. She needs clothes…underthings…shoes…everything."

"New relationship?" A twinkle of amusement danced in Candace's eyes.

"Very new."

"Well, tell me about her. What does she usually wear? Do you know her size?" Candace led him over to an area with casual clothes.

"She's small…but with curves that could kill a man," he replied without thinking and held out his hands to show Zoey's hip size. Candace's cheeks reddened but she studied his hands and nodded.

"Size eight, perhaps? How short?"

Connor tapped his hand to his chest. "Comes up to here exactly." He'd never forget that, not when she'd tilted her face up to look at him. The wariness and arousal warring with her past pain all there for him to see in such lovely eyes.

"Five-foot-four then?" Candace started pulling out pairs of jeans, checking sizes. She handed him a light and dark pair of jeans, then waved for him to follow her to a sweater rack. "You really should get her proper measurements, but I assume this is meant to be a surprise?"

"Yes."

Over the next hour, Candace helped him gather several pants, tops, a couple of coats, sneakers, boots and even a few strappy heels and a couple of fancy black dresses. Everything a young woman would need. She'd just informed him of their return policy in case the measurements were off when he remembered Zoey needed undergarments.

"What about…underclothes?" he asked Candace.

"Oh! I forgot." She ushered him to the lingerie section.

Connor's eyes nearly bugged out when he'd stared at the lacy thongs and sheer lingerie hanging on the mannequins. There were also flannel and silk pajamas as well as robes and slippers. His eyes kept drifting back to the see-through items.

Since when did women wear such… Christ, the last time he'd been with a woman such lacy, strappy things hadn't been nearly as enticing as these newer more revealing creations.

"Men usually buy the more revealing items, but…if I may give you some advice?"

Candace paused and Connor nodded.

"Keep your girlfriend warm. Buy something thick and soft for her."

Connor admitted the woman had a point. Zoey would look delicious in lingerie, but she'd freeze when she slept.

"Better go with the flannel," he said.

Candace smiled and started gathering a robe, slippers and flannel PJs before turning back to Connor.

"And the…sexy stuff?" She tried to hide a smile. Connor grinned back at her and pointed to the little red see-through garment that had a fringe of white fur on the edges of its short skirt.

"I want that."

"Lovely choice. The Christmas babydoll is always popular this time of year."

Connor could see why. The top part was practically transparent and would cup Zoey's breasts nicely, while the small red bikini bottom would reveal more of her glorious backside—a backside that he still ached to cup and mold and, Lord help him, smack it. *Hard*. She'd made such a sweet little moan when he'd done that last night.

His cock swelled at the thought, pressing against the front of his black wool pants. The damned thing seemed to have a mind of its own, thanks to Zoey.

He let Candace take him back to the checkout station and handed over his credit card. It had been ages since he'd had such a good time. Shopping for his woman had been entertaining. And she would be his woman. He stilled. His woman, but Ian's too. There was no way he could separate his friend from Zoey. They would share, like before with Lara. An old ache, one he so often tried to deny, burned a hole in his chest when he thought of Lara.

"Thank you, Candace. You've been very helpful." He took the

three large bags and winked at the shopping store clerk.

"You're very welcome, Mr. O'Shea." She handed him back his card. "Your girlfriend is a very lucky woman. She'll love the things you bought. I promise. *Any* woman would."

Assured by her words, Connor left the store grinning. The urge to get back home and shower Zoey with these gifts was so strong that he nearly used his preternatural speed to return to his car. The drive home took far too long. His usual patience evaporated long before he pulled into the driveway. The sun was below the horizon now, and the streetlights illuminated the nearby houses. The warmth of their glow mingled with those of the Christmas lights. He was struck by the beauty he'd taken for granted far too long. With a shake of his head, he turned back to the car.

Connor retrieved the shopping bags from the trunk, hurried to the garage door and ducked inside. He kicked the snow off his boots and headed to the living room. He ground to a halt when he saw Zoey curled up on the couch covered in a blanket. Lizzy, the tabby, lounged on Zoey's lap, little white-tipped paws kneading the blanket. Ian was in the kitchen staring at the bare cupboard with a scowl.

"There you are. You didn't answer your phone. We need groceries. Food." Ian's eyes dropped to the bags Connor carried. "But it seems you've been shopping already."

Connor walked over to Zoey and set the bags at her feet.

"I have. For Zoey." He let his voice caress the name as he'd done earlier when she'd melted into his kiss. Her eyes flicked from the bags up to his face.

"Oh... I couldn't... Whatever you bought you have to take it back." She tucked her feet up under the blanket, as though to get as far away as she could from the bags, like they were filled with poisonous snakes.

The anticipation that had been slowly building in his chest as he waited to see her pleasure died a swift death. His chest tightened and his features reverted to a mask of stone.

"I bought them for you." His tone was harsher than he'd meant it to be.

Her eyes narrowed and a flush of red accented her cheeks. "And I can't accept them. I have no way of repaying you."

Repay him? *Repay him?* What a stupid notion.

"I don't want your money." Again his tone had more of a bite than it should have.

"Oh, I see. You expect me to pay you some *other* way?" Her tart reply made him bare his teeth. His fangs slid down in anger.

"Bloody hell, woman, I would never expect you to… It's Christmas!" He snatched the bags up from the floor and marched off to his room. His pride was wounded, his good intentions sullied by her black assumptions. When he reached his room, he threw the bags down and slammed the door. The wood splintered a little as it crashed into the frame. The anger in him deflated, replaced by the empty pang of disappointment.

I was a fool to think I could show her I care…that I want her as much as Ian does.

He wished he could go back to yesterday, when he'd first laid eyes on her. If only he'd sent her away and never looked back. But she'd stayed and the walls of ice surrounding his heart were nearly melted through. She was a damned ray of sunlight determined to pierce him clear through his soul.

He'd done something nice, and she'd thrown it back in his face. Perhaps she wasn't the sweet, warm-hearted woman he'd believed her to be. Did she mean to play him against Ian? Or worse, she might want only Ian. He didn't want it to be true, he wanted…

Damn. He wanted *her,* just wanted her to like him the way she liked Ian.

But Zoey wasn't Lara. Zoey had rejected him and chosen Ian. There wasn't anything he could do to change that. He and Ian were like brothers, and he wouldn't fight to take a woman who didn't want him. There was only one thing left to do. He'd leave tonight and spend the holidays somewhere else until Zoey left his home.

What if she didn't leave? He couldn't come back if she was still here. His self-control was fraying and he wouldn't last if he had to be around Zoey and not have her. A heavy weight pressed on his chest. He was thankful, however briefly, he wasn't mortal, or else he'd have trouble breathing.

Connor sat on the edge of the bed, propped his elbows on his knees and covered his face with his hands, rubbing his eyes. A sigh of defeat escaped his lips.

Chapter Eight

"Not that I want to encourage you to choose him over me," Ian said slowly, "but you must believe Connor's intentions were good."

Guilt gnawed at Zoey's insides. She kept making mistakes, such big mistakes when it came to these two men.

"Even if he's just being kind, I can't take these things. I don't want to owe him."

"Zoey." The exasperation in Ian's tone was surprisingly thick. "Twas a gift. You can't owe someone for a gift. You need those clothes. I threw yours out because they were in a sorry state. You might as well take what Connor bought for you."

"You *threw out* my clothes?" She set Lizzy on the couch next to her and tossed the blanket off her body. As she jumped up, the edges of his buttonless shirt fluttered, threatening to fly open. She snatched the shirt ends and wrapped them tight around her. Grudgingly, she realized he had a point. She needed clothes.

Ian walked over to her and cupped her face with his palms.

"It's been thirty years since he's shown any interest in life. I was worried I was losing him, Zoey. He was turning more animal than man. But with you, I see the old Connor, my friend. He's trying to reach out and connect with you. Please let him, for my sake."

Ian's eyes were bright with emotions—love, regret, longing, and determination. He was asking her to share herself, at least a part of herself, with Connor because he loved the man like a brother and would do anything to save him, even share her.

It should have bothered her to think that a man would share her with his friend, but it didn't. She found it wondrous, sweet even, that the two of them would go so far in order to ensure the other's happiness. How many people could say they'd do the same?

Zoey's throat burned. "Okay," she agreed. Not for Ian's sake, but for Connor's. He needed her, more than Ian needed her, at least on some level. The realization that she could help him made her pride regarding his charity irrelevant.

Ian dropped his head and placed a kiss on her lips. "Thank you."

It burned like a well-kept fire by the hearth, a reassurance that he would be there when she returned. The parting of their lips was a tender thing, full of longing. When it ended, the flutter of lashes and the softening of his eyes became only a sweet memory as she turned down the hall and approached Connor's room. She rapped lightly on the door, using her free hand to hold her shirt together.

"Go away!" he bellowed. It would probably have been wise to leave him alone, but she didn't. Instead, she opened the door.

Connor sat on the edge of his bed, elbows propped on his knees, chin resting in one palm. He dropped his hands and stared at her as she entered. The glare on his face would have turned a less determined woman into stone. Zoey knelt at his feet by the shopping bags and looked up at him. A small black cat peeped out from under the large bed, yellow eyes wide and unblinking.

"*Mreow?*"

"Hush, Cleo. I'll make her go away," Connor promised. The cat slunk further back under the bed, vanishing from view. She appeared to be a sweet but timid thing.

Zoey ignored Connor's brusque tone. "Well? Aren't you going to show me what you bought?" Where she summoned the casual curiosity in her tone, she didn't know.

Connor glared at her.

"Fine. I'll just look myself." She reached for the bag closest to her. Connor snatched it from her hands.

"You said you didn't want them," he snapped. "You *rejected* them."

"And now I'm *un*rejecting them." She plucked the bag from his hands and set it down, reaching inside to pull out a pair of brown leather ankle boots and a couple of comfortable-looking jeans.

"You can't just unreject something," Connor growled. He

seemed to be under the foolish belief that his side of the argument had merit.

Zoey ignored him and stroked her fingertips over the butter-soft leather boots before raising her gaze to his with admiration.

"These are lovely." She meant it too. They were beautiful boots, and she couldn't wait to wear them. Hopefully, they fit.

Connor leaned forward, tore the boots from her hands and held them aloft.

"A pity you like them now, because you cannot have them. You cannot go around changing your mind."

Zoey rose to her feet and leapt at him to get the boots. "I'm a woman. We're allowed to."

He lifted the boots higher. When she jumped to reach them she fell into his body, knocking them both onto the bed. Connor groaned as she wriggled up him to get at the boots. When she slid back down, a hard bulge in his trousers rubbed against her. She fought off the wave of desire that swept through her with all the danger of a riptide.

"Easy, pet. You'll be the death of me." Connor dropped his head back onto the bed as she got off him, kneeling by the rest of the bags, her new boots clutched to her chest. She dared him with an aggressive stare to come after them again.

"What else did you get me?" She started pulling items out of the rest of the bags.

Connor gave in and watched her, quiet and pensive, his brown eyes dark with turbulent emotions. Zoey held up a bag, offering it to him.

"Would you like to show me what else you bought? I'd like to see. It was really very thoughtful. I'm sorry about what I said earlier. I've been on my own for too long. Everything has a price, usually one I'm not willing to pay. All of this is just so…insane. I mean, I got rescued by vampires who are buying presents. I think I'm allowed to overreact a little, right? Say you forgive me. Please, Connor." She peeped up at him, praying he'd forgive her for acting like a fool. His gesture really had been grand, and she'd been a fool to treat his kindness so suspiciously.

The hardness in Conner's eyes was not the least bit comforting. After a long moment, however, a hint of warmth returned. His eyes became like a fresh pot of brewed coffee, dark and hot.

"I'm sorry, lass, I reacted like a wounded bear. I should have been more understanding." He cleared his throat, then waved at the bags. "I bought a little of everything…" He took the bag she offered, pulling out a classy black cocktail dress that had a low dip in the back that would almost reach her backside if she were to wear it. Understated, yet incredibly sexy, just the way she wished to be when she pictured herself with a normal life. How had he known?

Sometime later, Zoey sat back on her heels, surrounded by a small mountain of clothes. Only one bag remained untouched, a small red bag with fancy tissue paper. Her fingers caught the handles at the same time Connor's did.

"Oh, that's not for you—"

"But…"

"Go on, Connor. Let her open it." From the doorway, Ian peered in, his tone more dangerous and seductive than it had ever been before. A knowing grin crossed his lips. He leaned against the doorjamb, wearing only a pair of faded blue jeans, the top button undone. Something about that, the half-dressed man in front of her, sent shivers through her. These men would surely drive her mad. Her perception of both of them was changing. She should take neither man lightly. Like it or not, she was at their mercy.

"Go on, Zoey, open it," Ian encouraged. His look was almost feline and highly predatory, as though he hungered at the sight of her.

Her hands shook as she removed the tissue and brushed over something soft and furry. She gripped the item and pulled it out of the sack. It was a babydoll, a thin red piece of lingerie, the hem of the flowing skirt-like top lined with white fur.

"Oh!" Her lips parted with a little gasp.

Connor's face paled, and he tugged at the collar of his black sweater.

"I'll take it back," he muttered and reached for it.

Zoey shook her head and clasped the lingerie to her chest. "No! I like it. I've just never worn something like this…before." The blush that followed her breathless words must have reached the roots of her hair.

"I wouldn't worry. You won't be in it long." Ian's dark promise sent a shiver through her. Zoey didn't know what to say to that. She swallowed and gathered the mountain of clothes and stood.

"Thank you, Connor. These are wonderful." *You are wonderful,* nearly spilled out as well. The last thing she needed was to make a spectacle of herself by revealing how much she liked him. How much she liked them both.

"You're welcome." His gruff reply made her smile for some reason.

"You should shower and change," Ian said. "We can go out when you're done." She nodded and tried to slide past him through the doorway, rubbing against him as she passed. A riot of heat spiked through her when his masculine scent and the barest hint of aftershave drifted beneath her nose. Her body flushed, eager to finish what every one of his kisses had promised her.

Zoey forced herself to flee to the bathroom and escape the temptation Ian presented. She needed time to gather her thoughts and steel herself against the advances the two vampires made against her. She had to be sure her mind was her own. Knowing what she knew now about their glamour, and how it affected her reaction to them, it was easy to doubt what she was feeling. They were sex on a stick to her, but was that actually how she felt? Or just a chemical manipulation of her body reacting to them? The last thing she wanted, the last thing she could afford, was to be swept away by her hormones and getting confused about what was real. If she had time to think with some distance, she might be able to figure out what she really felt about Ian and Connor.

———•———

NONE OF THE TREES IN the lot were right. They were all too perfect, too flawless. A Christmas tree ought to have character and be unique. Zoey rubbed her new mittens together and glanced around, looking for her pair of tall Irish vampires. She couldn't help but smile when she spotted them hovering at the back of the lot, shoulders touching as they stared at something she couldn't see. Zoey attempted to sneak up on them, trying not to laugh.

""Tis the sorriest looking twig I've ever seen," Ian said to Connor.

"More like driftwood than a tree," Connor agreed. "What do you think, Zoey?"

So much for being sneaky. They hadn't even glanced in her direction. Zoey put her hands on their shoulders and gently nudged them apart so she could what they were looking at.

"It's perfect!"

"You must be joking," Connor said.

But she wasn't, and she couldn't stop smiling. Clearly neither of them had ever watched *A Charlie Brown Christmas*. It was the perfect tree. More like a large, five-foot high twig with some misplaced branches.

"Can we get this one?" she pleaded. Ian and Connor's mouths opened slightly.

"Really?" they asked in unison.

"Of course! My father always said that the perfect tree was the one that was unique, different. The saddest looking trees are usually the ones with the most character." Zoey stepped up to the tree and reached out to touch the nearest branches.

"It looks a bit like Ian's—"

Ian silenced Connor with a light blow to his stomach.

Zoey ignored them as the two vamps tussled like overgrown boys; she looked instead at the tree. The pine needles feathered over the thick wool of her mitten. So many memories of other Christmases, ones that were bittersweet to recall. Her mother at home with chili cooking in the crockpot, while Zoey and her father made the annual trip to the tree lot to find the right tree. God, she'd missed the heavy scent of evergreen.

She bit her bottom lip to stop it from trembling. Her breath caught in her throat. It was all too much, too soon. She turned away and bumped into Ian's chest. His arms curled around her, pulling her into his body. The sobs came, and though quiet, they wracked her body.

"Shhh…" Ian soothed.

"Ah, it means that much to you…" Connor muttered from somewhere behind her. "We'll get the twig…er…tree."

A laugh bubbled in her throat, and she stared up at Ian. Connor was right behind her, so near that she was suddenly, intensely aware of how close all three of them had become. It struck her in that moment that the three of them felt right. She shared the intimate space with them and there was no awkwardness, no competition or concerns. She'd been so worried and ashamed for wanting them both before, but the temptation was too great to resist. Why should she fight something that felt so right?

She wiped her eyes with her sleeve and managed a watery smile.

"My dad and I used to buy the least perfect tree on the lot. It was our tradition." She looked away, shy and a little embarrassed by her reaction. "I wasn't prepared for how sad it made me, to be here without him."

Ian stroked her hair back from her face and brushed a kiss over her forehead.

"Let's make a new tradition then. Connor, get the tree."

———◆———

TWO HOURS LATER, ZOEY WAS sitting in a lawn chair in the driveway laughing as Connor and Ian argued about how to rig up the Christmas lights on the roof. The two century-old vampires couldn't agree on traditional lights or icicle lights.

"Zoey, love, tell Connor here that these are more appropriate…" Ian came toward her, holding a string of traditional lights.

Connor growled and tripped Ian as he passed by. Ian face-planted in the snow, only to jump up and leap at his friend like an animal. The two men wrestled like tiger cubs. Zoey wasn't worried; she heard laughing amidst their scuffling.

"Calm down, you two! Go with the icicle lights." Both men stilled. Ian had Connor in a head lock. They both raised their heads, reluctant grins on their faces.

"Fine. Icicles it is. You can make it up to me later, Zoey. But I only accept payments in kisses." Ian winked.

Zoey blushed all the way to her toes. The idea had a little too much appeal, and she was sure she'd happily get herself deep into debt.

"Let's go inside and warm up," Conner said. "Well, those of us who need to. We'll finish the lights tomorrow." He and Ian stood up and brushed snow off their clothes.

The house was warm and merry. The tree by the window was lit up and covered with shiny balls and various ornaments that the three of them had hung before going outside to put up the Christmas lights. Music drifted through the air along with the scent of nutmeg and gingerbread.

It was everything she loved about the holidays, and even though she missed her parents, being here with Ian and Connor somehow felt just as special. A new memory to add to the old. Never in a thousand years would she have guessed she'd be spending Christmas with two handsome immortals, each determined to seduce her and care for her at the same time. She doubted any other woman would be as lucky as she was tonight.

A naughty idea tiptoed feather light into her mind. She bit her bottom lip to hide the smile it gave her. Was she brave enough to do it? Was she ready? She shot a glance at Ian and Connor. Connor was stretched out, feet propped up over one arm of the couch, hands clasped behind his head, looking relaxed for perhaps the first time as he watched *A Christmas Story* on the TV. Ian was busy in the kitchen putting away the leftovers from their dinner in the fridge.

A stirring of hope filled her chest. She wanted to fit into their world, to be a part of both their lives, and sharing them was one way to start. It had worked with them once before, and did she really mind the idea of having them both? Was that somehow being greedy? Perhaps after having nothing, a little greed wasn't such a bad thing.

With a grin and a touch of nerves, she went to find the red

babydoll.

Chapter Nine

Zoey checked her appearance in the bathroom mirror. Nervousness fluttered inside her with the chaos of a swarm of butterflies trapped inside a net. She could do this. She *wanted* to do this. She just prayed things would work out. Choosing between Ian and Connor was not an option. It was so clear how close these two men had always been, like brothers. Loving one without loving the other would drive a wedge between them and ultimately drive them apart.

Please let them both want me enough to share me. They'd shared Lara, after all. Could they be the same with her? Even if she wasn't a true mate, she wanted to prove to them she could love them both equally, because she did. How it was possible in just a few days she didn't know, but she did.

She loved the way Connor hid his sweetness beneath a gruff demeanor, and how he never restrained his passion when he was with her. And she loved Ian's tender-hearted smiles and irresistibly seductive kisses. Both had an adorable way of trying to give her everything she wanted and needed, like it was coded in their ancient DNA to care for their woman. It was time she showed them how much they meant to her.

She stepped out of the bathroom and walked down the hall, all too aware of the carpet beneath her bare feet. The two men, *her* two men, stood in the kitchen sipping coffee, studying the small village of gingerbread houses they'd made earlier that evening. Much to her dismay, Ian and Connor had made an elaborate castle with a moat being attacked by a dragon, while she'd opted for a traditional little house that looked pathetically plain next to it.

Connor said something, pointing to her house, and Ian burst into a rich laugh. They seemed so comfortable with each other now, so different from that first night when they were ready to rip each other's throats out. The strain between them was gone, that tension reduced to a bad memory.

Ian was the first to catch sight of her. His coffee mug crashed onto the floor. Connor turned and caught his breath, then grinned.

"It looks so much better on you than the hanger." Even though his words were quiet, they struck her like a shot of warm brandy.

Zoey smoothed her hands over the red babydoll and tried to will away her self-consciousness. She'd been naked around both of them, had kissed them and done much more with much less on than this piece of lingerie. She wanted to be sexy and wild with them. Maybe it wouldn't matter if she had only a little sexual experience compared to these men who'd lived for two centuries. They'd probably slept with hundreds of beautiful perfect woman in that time. She hoped she could measure up. There was so much passion in her right now she felt ready to burst.

Ian nudged the remnants of the coffee mug aside with the toe of his boot. "Do I get to collect my kisses now?"

"Don't frighten her," Connor whispered as he started to prowl toward her.

Ian also approached, but in a far more casual way. "You're doing a good enough job of that yourself. You're not on a nature documentary, you know. She's not a wildebeest."

For the first time since meeting them, Zoey truly felt like the prey she always knew she was to the vampires. A walking Happy Meal. The hungry looks they gave her were evidence that they'd eat her up if given half the chance. In a good way, of that she had not doubt, but she also knew that she might end up getting bitten again. She had to trust they could control their natures with her in the height of their passion.

Ian reached her first, his palms cupping her shoulders. His skin felt cool against her heated flesh, but not as cool as before. His green eyes were warm and bright, like grass on a summer's day.

"Tell me you won't choose just one of us." Ian's tone was urgent and barely above a growl. "You can handle us both, can't you?" She knew he didn't just mean physically, but emotionally as well.

A second set of hands, Connor's, slid around her hips from behind as they trapped her between their tall, firm bodies. Zoey shut her eyes and nodded, more to herself than either of them.

"Yes. I want to be with you. Both of you." There. She'd said it. Now what was she supposed to do?

She turned to look over her shoulder at Connor. Some silent communication seemed to pass between them.

"My bed or yours?" he asked at last.

"Mine tonight, yours the next." Ian gave Zoey a look so scorching she wondered how she didn't get burned.

"Is that okay with you, Zoey?" Ian cupped her cheek and watched her reaction closely.

"Yes…"

Connor slid his hand around hers, the grip comforting as he led her down the hall, Ian following behind them. Once inside, Connor shut the door and leaned back against it. Zoey looked between the two and wrapped her arms around her waist nervously.

"Look, I don't know how to start this. Will somebody just kiss me?" She felt like an idiot asking like that, but it was what she needed.

Ian's voice became a deep, honeyed rumble. "As you wish."

He grasped her face in his hands and leaned in until his lips touched hers. Every worry, every fear faded away. Ian could do that to her—ease her anxiety and yet still melt her inside with his touch. His lips moved over hers, delicate, teasing, tasting. She responded, lost in the rhythm of their mouths. Ian's tongue sought a playful dance with hers. Zoey moaned with pleasure. A single kiss, long and sensual, was all she needed to come alive. She opened her eyes long enough to see Connor still leaning against the closed doors, arms crossed.

"Show him your passion, Zoey." Connor's whisper betrayed his own hunger to join them. A wicked smile flirted with the edges of his lips.

"Yes, show me, love." Ian forced her back a few steps until she bumped into the bed.

His hips pinned hers against the mattress. He smoothed his hands down her back, over the swell of her backside, the bikini bottom barely a barrier to the cool skin of his palms. Her flesh burned with his erotic touch. He gripped her ass, jerking her up against him so her feet left the ground. She wrapped her arms around his neck, hanging on as he raised her up to set her on the edge of the bed. Ian urged her to crawl back toward the headboard and he followed, coming down over her body. His hands gently pried her shaking knees apart as he settled into the cradle of her thighs.

"You all right?" he whispered before kissing her. It was a soft brush, a little caress of reassurance, and it relaxed her instantly.

"I'm fine. It's just been a few years since I…" She bit her lip and looked in Connor's direction. She saw him push away from the door and step toward her.

"You'll be fine, love. We're here to please you, aren't we, Connor?" Ian kissed the corner of her mouth and then trailed his mouth up to her ear, licking inside.

A sharp pang of lust hit her womb and traveled like lightning up her spine back to her ear. She arched with a hiss as he repeated the erotic licking, and the folds of her sex throbbed with hot desire. Ian continued the wicked torture of her ear, rocking his still clothed body against hers, until she'd dissolved into a puddle of incoherent desire.

Then he relented, just as she was on the verge of coming. He sat back on the bed and removed his sweater, tossing it aside. Zoey gazed up at him, trembling with vulnerability and hunger as he loomed over her, his palms settling into the comforter on either side of her head. She shivered and watched as he slid down her body until his face hovered above her mound. When he hooked his thumbs in her bikini bottoms and tugged them down her legs, she clamped her eyes shut, suddenly shy. What would he think of her? She'd never had a man go down on her before.

"Open your eyes, Zoey." It was Connor's voice next to her ear. Her lashes fanned up and saw him on the edge of the bed next to her, watching her. His dark eyes glittered, wild and savage.

Ian pulled her legs apart, tapping behind her knees and she bent them without thinking, setting her heels in the bed, allowing Ian to stare down at her. She tore her gaze away from Connor only to see Ian's green eyes flash with a strange sheen of crimson.

"I'm dying to taste you," Ian growled in a voice so low that she felt its vibration more than she heard the words. His palms slid down her inner thighs and she threw her head back against the pillow. Her body convulsed when Ian's thumbs rubbed slow patterns along the skin of her legs, just inches from her core.

Connor now demanded her attention, cupping her cheek and turning her to face him.

"Kiss me," he purred, then stoked her lips with a mind-numbing kiss—the sort that stole a woman's heart and soul. Like a first and last kiss and every one in between. It had a certain magic that could hold a woman frozen in time, bound by a mix of love and passion. Zoey's eyes singed with tears as she tried to return the power of the moment, reflect some of that intensity back to Connor, to show him she felt the same as he did.

She never got the chance, because Ian kissed the top of her mound and nibbled his way down. Her hands flailed as she tried to find his shoulders, his hair, anything to grasp on to as he licked her slit.

Connor swallowed her scream of riotous pleasure as Ian continued to taste her. Something jerked her arms above her head, pinning them firmly out of the way. Zoey forced her eyes open again. Connor had captured her wrists and was keeping her distracted while Ian played between her legs.

Thoughts couldn't form, words wouldn't come, there was only wave after wave of building, aching pleasure as she strained to reach the climax she desperately needed. She was helpless against the two of them, only able to accept whatever they gave her. Years of anxiety had wound her tighter than a cork in a bottle and she was so close to bursting free.

"Please…Ian…let me come. God…just let me come!" she begged, breathless between Connor's kisses.

Ian's breath tickled her inner thigh as he licked and nibbled his way to her knee. She wanted to scream in frustration as the desire inside her continued to be left unfulfilled.

"What do you think, Connor? Should we grant her wish?" He smoothed his hands up and down her thighs, rubbing her sensitive skin, but she needed his mouth back on her clit, or better yet, his cock deep inside her.

"Connor…" she whispered, meeting his eyes with a desperate look.

There was a wildness in his gaze, and she glimpsed the predator he'd tried to hide tonight. He seemed to revel in her echoing need for release. His grip on her wrists tightened and he dropped his head to nip her lower lip. She arched in his arms, and both men chuckled.

"Take her slow, Ian. Make her work for it." His dark voice stirred her senses and made her heady with anticipation.

Ian sat back and Zoey was treated to a fresh view of his chest and the way his muscles flexed as he shrugged out of his jeans. His cock sprang forward and she wanted to stroke the massive length of it.

He came forward again, cupped her ass, lifted her up and then with one hand guided the tip of his shaft into her. Zoey held still, even though she wanted more than anything to squirm in eagerness.

While Ian began to press into her an inch at a time, Connor tore the spaghetti straps of the babydoll's top and ripped open the sheer bodice, baring her breasts. He filled his hand with one, pinching and rolling the beaded nipple between his thumb and forefinger while his mouth settled over the other peak.

Her body flushed, then she screamed as Ian thrust into her. He stretched her to the breaking point and she thought she might die from the sudden mix of pleasure and pain. Ian withdrew, leaving an awful empty feeling in its wake. Seconds later, he was driving back into her, surging deeper. He groaned at the same moment she did when he thrust to the hilt.

"Christ, you're so tight," Ian's accent grew thicker than she'd ever heard before and it made her inner walls clench around him. A wildness filled her.

"Harder!"

Connor lifted his head, shared a cat-like smile with Ian. "She's been a good lass, give it to her."

And he did. Ian gripped her hips as he took Zoey to the edge at a pounding pace. Connor moved back, his palms cupping her face as he gazed down at her. Zoey looked back and forth between the two. Beneath the hunger, the desire, their eyes were filled with softer emotions, ones she felt as well, and she was mesmerized by it.

Finally it was too much. She surrendered, her back bowing up off the bed as her climax took her. Stars dotted her vision—the white hot intensity of her union with Ian shaking her to the very foundation of her soul as she came. She was barely aware of Ian's own roar of satisfaction. Her fell body limp and sated as she felt Ian withdraw from her.

"Ian?" she asked, trying to keep her eyes open.

"Shhh…" he whispered from somewhere beside her. "Rest a bit."

Even wanting to stay awake, her body craved sleep and she obeyed and immediately slipped into a deep, dreamless sleep.

———◆———

ZOEY WOKE A FEW HOURS later to Connor's teasing kisses. Her eyes opened briefly as she returned his kiss, curling her arms around his neck.

"Are you ready for me now?" he asked, his accent thick yet soft, making her body shiver.

"Mmmm," she moaned in answer, kissing him again. The blankets were pulled from her body and he was moving between her thighs, right where she wanted him.

"Zoey, lass," he groaned as he raised her hips, taking him inside her. "Christ, woman!" he hissed and thrust harder, burying himself completely. Once again she was filled to a near breaking point, but it felt wonderful.

"She feels good, doesn't she?" Ian chuckled from the nearby darkness.

Connor's laugh turned to a curse as he sank into her again. Zoey loved having all of him inside her, possessing her in a way she hadn't thought possible. Knowing Ian was watching only made her blood run hotter, her own arousal spike. Connor gripped her knee, pulling it tight to his hip, molding them together.

She thrashed her head against the pillow as he took her, body and soul. "Connor…God…that feels so good…" Both of them had her, all of her. She could only pray they'd be merciful and remember she was just a mortal. She screamed in pleasure. Connor collapsed on top of her, panting against her neck. He licked her skin even as her inner muscles clamped around his cock.

He nibbled her ear. "Hmm. Mind if I have a wee bite?"

She giggled.

Ian shoved Connor's shoulder. "Now, Connor, you greedy bastard, I've not had the chance to taste her yet." Conner rolled dramatically off Zoey and then Ian was pulling her over his body. She rested her chin to his chest, boneless, shutting her eyes. She was vaguely aware of Ian lifting one of her arms to his mouth and nibbled playfully.

"One taste?" he asked. "I want to know you, Zoey. Please let me taste you." She opened one eye and stared at him. "Drinking from you will let me see inside your heart, your mind."

"Will it hurt?" she asked. The last time she'd been bitten it had been when she was beyond aroused, but now she was sated, and more aware of herself. She didn't mind that this would let him see into her. She had nothing to hide from him.

Connor leaned over beside her and kissed her shoulder. It felt so good to lie there with them both, exploring, delighting in their appetites.

"It might sting at first, but if you relax, it will ease."

Zoey wasn't frightened, but the intimacy of giving her blood was something she'd never expected to face.

"Okay." She drew a breath as his fangs slid out and he bit into her wrist. She tensed as the sting sharpened.

Connor touched her cheek. "Relax, pet," he said, turning her face toward him.

Sharing blood with Ian, just as when Connor had tasted her, formed some mystical connection between them. Invisible strings seemed to weave her and Ian together—two souls, nearly merged.

"Tell me something about you, Zoey," said Conner. "Before the accident, what were your plans?"

Zoey rested her face against Connor's cool palm, watching his lips move as he spoke. Ian sucked at her wrist a second longer then licked the wound closed. He stroked her hair, the gentleness of the motion making her feel warm and safe.

She turned and rested her cheek on his chest.

"Before… I wanted to be a photographer. I was good at art, loved to sketch, but what I really loved was taking pictures. I was enrolled in photography classes. After the accident, I had to drop out of art school and sell the house. There were so many expenses. Eventually I even had to pawn my camera…"

Her words died as emotions began to clog her throat. Selling that camera had been like the last bell tolling in a cemetery, reminding her she had to give up her dreams. It was all dead now, every hope she had for that future. She jerked away and started to sit up. Ian rolled, pinning her beneath him on the bed.

"No, lass, you can't shut us out."

"Too late for that," Connor added.

She rubbed at her eyes, wiping away fresh tears. She looked away from them around the room, noticing the lovely pictures on the walls.

"When I first woke up here, I thought I was dead. The room was filled with pictures of places I've never been."

"Ian took those. He likes to snap a picture every now and then. He even set up the camera on timers to get shots during the day that he couldn't manage in person. It's a bit of a passion for him too. We'll take you with us, when we travel next," Connor promised.

Zoey wanted to cry even harder. He made it sound so natural, so *normal* that she'd be with them. But this wasn't going to last forever. How could it?

Ian slid off her so that she was nestled between their bodies. "Er…Zoey. We'd like to talk to you about something."

She forced herself to smile, but it was brittle. She feared the worst. "Yes?"

"What would you say if Connor and I asked you to stay past

Christmas? We've grown quite fond of you, and neither of us wishes for you to leave. Now—" He pressed a finger against her lips before she could protest. "We know you've got your pride, and this has nothing to do with charity."

Connor echoed the tender look Ian gave her with a slow caress, rubbing her stomach and tracing the spot where she'd been stabbed. How did he know where to touch her? The scars were all but gone, and had been mere hours after she'd woken up in their home.

It was madness to even consider their offer, but she couldn't resist. She was hopelessly in love with them. Any excuse to stay was worth considering. "I have to support myself, if I stay…"

"What if," Ian said slowly as though trying to carefully convince her of his words. "You return to your classes, get your degree and open a studio? We could be investors. Right?"

"We could," Connor agreed instantly and sat up next to her in bed. "Investments are how we get by these days. We want you to stay."

That surprised her and filled her with a sense of hope. It scared the hell out of her. They wanted her to stay. She wanted to stay. But she had to be sure it was the right thing to do.

"I'll think about it."

"Good." Ian kissed her and soon both men were tucking her beneath the covers as sleep took over. No nightmares could take away the sense of peace and safety these two had given her in that moment.

CHAPTER TEN

THE CATHEDRAL WAS BEAUTIFUL. THE massive stained glass windows glowed with candlelight from within. Multicolored shadows splashed over the snow below the glass like a frozen kaleidoscope. The gothic spires of the old edifice rose up into the clear midnight sky, majestic and mysterious. A pair of ten-foot tall archangels guarded the entrance, their wings curved around their shoulders, heads bowed as though in mourning.

Zoey held her breath, taking in the old world splendor from across the street.

The last week had passed quickly, too quickly for her. Wrapped up in her new intimate life with Ian and Connor, she'd lost all track of time. Like staring into a snow globe and imagining herself far away from the cares of the world in a tiny house, flakes of snow swirling around her. The past few days had been an endless dream full of delight and wonder. Between the erotic nights spent in the arms of her men and exploring the city without a care, she'd found herself. They'd helped her live again, not just exist.

The church doors opened. Light spilled across the icy walkway, painting the frozen water a rich gold, like the midmorning sun striking a river's surface. Goosebumps rose on Zoey's forearms, and she rubbed them through her thick winter coat. The sight before her humbled and moved her in a way she hadn't felt since before her parents died.

The building was filled with life as the parishioners inside began to sing. The night breeze pulled the notes out into the air around her like an unseen choir of angels. The sounds of elation and love were wondrous. She felt like a child again, as if hearing music for the first time. Then the feeling of something greater stirred inside her bones, demanding to be recognized.

Faith. It had been so long since she'd believed in anything. She'd lost her faith and faith in herself…but no longer. A gasp of joy escaped her in a foggy puff of breath and she laughed.

It was nearly midnight and mass would start soon. She saw Connor and Ian at the back of the parking lot, still talking by the car. They'd join her soon, but it wouldn't hurt to run inside and grab some seats. She checked the street and stepped off the curb to cross. She slipped a few times as she reached the middle. The road was covered in black ice, and she knew full well how dangerous it was. Her clutch purse slipped from her hands, and Zoey knelt to pick it up.

A car turned onto the street, tires whining as it tried to right itself. The driver accelerated and the headlights flashed onto Zoey a second too late. She scrambled awkwardly, trying to gain traction. The driver hit the brakes and the car fishtailed out of control.

The purse fell from her hands as the car struck her.

As though she were in a dream, everything that followed seemed not to be happening to her, but to some other poor soul. She could only stand by and watch.

Bones shattered, organs were crushed, her breath was stolen as she flew fifteen feet away. She slid over the ice like a broken ragdoll and then stopped. Everything went numb except her face. One cheek was pressed against the freezing ice and it burned like fire.

She was facing the church and the bells in the tower above her began to sway. They tolled loud and clear as the midnight hour struck and Christmas Eve turned to Christmas Day. The screams of the people nearby were drowned out beneath the merry clamor of bells. They were all she could hear and she clung to that sound, fighting to stay conscious.

Zoey sought to make sense of the shapes and movement before her. Most were blurry silhouettes against the pale light from the church's entrance. The stone angel on the right was the only thing she could truly see. Everything else was too confusing, too dark. The angel's head was bowed, its gown rippling around its legs, pulled by an ancient wind strong enough to move stone.

Then the massive feathered wings, once shrouded in grief around its body, suddenly flung wide. Diamonds glittered on the wing tips as the stone cracked and splintered. White fire shot through the fracturing stone. It was the most beautiful thing she'd ever seen. The angel shivered, and the stone dust covering it blew away. The explosion of light that followed, bathed Zoey in its fiery heat, and she let go.

————◆————

"DO YOU THINK SHE'LL LIKE it?" Ian asked Connor as they stood by the car. People passed them on the way to mass, laughing and filled with holiday cheer. It used to make him sad to see such joy, but now he was full of happiness as well and the mood of these people was an added blessing.

"You're sure it's the one she pawned?" Connor studied the camera Ian had handed him that they'd hidden in a new camera bag in the back of the car.

"I saw the shop's name when we bonded, and this camera. It's either hers or one just like it." Ian tucked the delicate piece of equipment back into the bag and set it in the backseat, next to the other presents they'd purchased that evening.

Ian hadn't told Zoey yet about the bridge between their minds. It was something he planned to tell her soon. From the moment he touched her a week ago, he'd known she was his true mate, and Connor's. She belonged to him and Connor just as Lara had. It made one wonder if there was in fact such a thing as reincarnation. They were fortunate to have been given a second chance at finding someone who would bring them close to being human again.

He wasn't sure if she'd been aware of the subtle changes: their human appetites, their warmer skin, the occasional need to breathe. It had been happening to both him and Connor, just as they remembered what it had been like with Lara. A wondrous sense of life. Zoey was the woman he wished to build his future on. She was his salvation.

"She'll love it." Connor gave a boyish grin as he turned toward the church. "We'd best get inside before mass starts."

"Try not to vamp out this time. It always causes a panic." Ian shook his head, laughing.

Connor smirked. "You do that one time for a laugh and get branded for life. I thought the good Father would have enjoyed a livening up of the Christmas mass." He'd flashed a bit of fang and fiery eye just for fun back in the 1840s. It had not been well received by the presiding priest.

"We almost *were* branded. And staked."

"Come on. Father Callahan was the most boring priest in Irish history. We saved those people from dying of boredom."

"And had to move to America as a result."

The sound of screeching tires interrupted their conversation.

Ian's instincts died. He was rooted to the spot, watching helplessly as a car spun out of control and hit someone standing in the middle of the street. A woman. He heard the impact crush her body and the shocked, pained exhalation as she fell to the ground.

A last breath, one he'd heard so often in his nightmares of late. A sound that would follow him forever into the shadows of the valley of death.

"Zoey!" Connor's voice was distant, as though it were underwater.

Zoey? That couldn't be Zoey, not her. Not her.

They ran to the body. The body. She was barely more than that. Her soul was leeching away. Blood dripped from her lips onto the icy road. Her eyes were half-closed. Life still glimmered in their luminous depths, gazing at something he couldn't see. He followed her line of sight and saw only a large stone angel in the churchyard, flakes of snow swirling around its bowed head and wings.

Connor was on his knees, checking her injuries. The crowd around them were calling for help and dialing 911. When Connor raised his head and met Ian's eyes, they spoke without words.

She's nearly gone. Not long now.

It had happened once before, watching the life leave the woman they'd loved. They'd been unable to stop it then. Lara had slipped away. There one minute and gone in the next, final breath. Life was such a delicate thing, so many ways it could end. Each breath, each beat of a human heart was a gift, one so often taken for granted.

Connor's voice broke. "Ian, I *cannot* do this again."

Ian's chest seized as he saw Connor's face. He was fully human in that instant. They both were. Grief, loss and love were not for immortal hearts, or so he'd believed. After eighty years, he'd thought he'd never be able to feel this way again. Zoey had changed them, brought them back their humanity. Ian would be damned if he let her slip away.

"Grab Zoey. Let's get her home!" Ian shouted.

They had no time, not if they were going to save her. Connor picked Zoey up in his arms and headed straight for home, moving like lightning, leaving a bewildered crowd behind him.

❧

CONNOR BURST INTO HIS ROOM and laid Zoey on his bed, barely breathing. She looked so beautiful, even as she lingered so close to death. Ian appeared in the doorway a moment later, face pale.

"We'll turn her." It was not a question.

Connor nodded. At first he'd meant to protest, but looking at her now he was in total agreement with Ian. They had to save her. They bit their wrists and took turns giving her their blood.

If they succeeded she might hate them, but they had to take that chance. So long as Zoey was alive, or at least as alive as one of their kind could ever be, he could never regret the decision. Maybe someday she'd forgive them. After several long minutes, they stopped and waited. Her body shuddered, one last breath released so softly that Connor barely heard it.

"Zoey…" Pain flooded from his breaking heart.

"Were we too late?" Shock carved lines in Ian's face as he knelt by the bed.

"We can't be… She can't… not again. She *can't* go now."

Even as much as he wanted to believe he could deny fate, Connor knew that mysterious forces in the vast universe sometimes took control. Perhaps the angels had wanted Zoey, and they'd come to claim her. How could he, an immortal cursed to live on blood, argue his right to keep her? He didn't deserve her, and neither did Ian. Maybe they were monsters after all. Monsters didn't get happy endings.

Ian dropped his head into his hands, shaking with silent sobs. They'd failed. Connor sat down next to the still body. His chest quaked as he struggled to draw breath, as though he was dying along with her. Of all the times he'd longed for death, had stared into the obsidian waters of the river night, it was nothing compared to now, except perhaps when he'd seen Seamus standing over Lara's dead body. It had happened again, the thing that made his dead heart stir to life in his chest was gone.

"Oh lass, you always were too good for the likes of us." Connor stroked her hair back from her face, his eyes burning with tears he couldn't shed.

His eyes closed and she was still there, haunting him. He could see her brilliant smile, the one that lit her face with a strange and wondrous magic. Connor's hands clenched. He could almost feel her small hand in his, his fingers lacing with hers as though she'd been made for him. The memory was strong, and it broke his heart all over again. Without Zoey he was nothing…

Just one more moment, holding her in his arms, if he could only have her back. Long enough to tell her everything in his heart.

—◆—

THE HOUSE WAS QUIET. ZOEY'S parents were cuddled up on the couch, the TV screen showing *It's a Wonderful Life*. Zoey sat by the fire, a blanket around her as she watched her parents talk softly to each other. Her father smiled and her mother laughed, whispering something in his ear.

Her father turned, confusion crossed his face as he saw her.

"Zoey, what are you doing here?"

"It's Christmas," she replied with a bright smile and got up.

Her mother's eyes shone with a bittersweet shimmer. "Go back, Zoey."

The words stung. She belonged here, didn't she? With them. Something pulled at her stomach, a cramping pain that made her double over.

She raised her head. "Dad…I want to stay with you…"

Her father shook his head sadly. They were her family, her life, why did they not want her here?

"We are always with you, sweetheart. Never forget that. But you can't stay. Your place is back there, with them."

Them? "No…Dad please…" Tears sparked in her eyes, and she rubbed her fists against them.

"Zoey, you've lived so long with your suffering. It's time to accept the joy of the life you've been given. Our chapter is ended. That book is on the shelf. But you still have a story to live, one all your own."

Her parents came over, kneeling on either side of her and hugged her tight. That feeling of closeness burned into her heart and mind, like the last kiss given by a lover, or the final wave from a departing friend. Sorrow and grief shared space in her heart with the memories of better, brighter days. Her mother stroked the hair back from her face.

"We love you, wherever you go, whatever you do. We are with you. Now go. Live the life destiny has given you."

The sharp pain struck her stomach again, and her parents faded into a gentle mist that rose up from the ground.

———◆———

A SPARK SKITTERED THROUGH CONNOR'S FINGERS where they'd touched Zoey's cheek. His eyes flew open as the spark whipped through his hand where it had contact with her skin. It was a spark he recognized. Of life, after a fashion.

"Zoey?" Hope fluttered within him like a dove with newly

mended wings. The pulsing of Zoey's flesh grew sharper and stronger as that immortal spark took hold of her.

They'd done it.

"Christ, Ian, she's going to make it!" Connor nearly whooped with joy. Ian lifted his tear strained face and reached for Zoey's limp hand by the edge of the bed.

"We did it!"

Everything would be all right now. As long as she could forgive them…

"We did it."

———

"ZOEY…" THE VOICE SHE HEARD was raw with pain. She knew that voice, yet she didn't know it.

"Zoey, we love you. You cannot leave us. Do you hear me, woman?" Another voice growled.

"Find your way back, I can't lose you," the first voice whispered.

Cool fingers stroked her flesh and the sensation was startling, amazing, like an electric surge to her system. A flash of violent pain shuddered through her and she let out a cry. Her body seized. She couldn't stop the rolling waves of pain. Bones snapped into place, flesh, tissue seemed to pull back together. Every second was pure agony and she couldn't do anything but shout and writhe. Tears and sobs came without control.

"Zoey, let it go. Let it all out."

She surrendered, letting the emotions and the physical pain spiral through her. After several seconds it faded and she was still—utterly still except for an occasional tremble. Her eyes fluttered open as she took in the scene around her.

She was lying in Connor's bed. Connor. She knew him, loved him. And Ian. She loved him too. Her two great loves sat on either side of her, their eyes wide with worry, tension stretching their mouths into tight lines.

"Thank God." Ian's tone was full of reverence and relief.

Zoey tried to move, her body was limp and sore, as though she'd been beaten all over.

"What happened?" she asked, her voice cracking with pain. Her vision sharpened, the fabric of the comforter beneath her fingertips whispered under her skin, the feeling so strong, so…sensual. Her body was different. It felt alien in so many ways and yet right.

"You died," Connor answered bluntly, eyes dark as tree bark in winter.

Ian shot him a baleful glare. "Tact, Connor." He turned back to Zoey. "Do you remember the car hitting you?"

The memory returned with shocking clarity—the sudden impact and breaking of her body…and then it all was muddled after that.

"Connor and I…we turned you." Ian looked away and cleared his throat. "We couldn't lose you, Zoey. We'd been through that once before. A world without you was a world we couldn't live in. I hope you can forgive us. We made the choice without you, and I'd vowed I'd never do that. But you're ours, a true mate, just like I told you about. You remember?"

She stared up at them, amazed at this new brighter sight she had. Vampire vision? Connor took her face in his hands, stroking her cheeks with his thumbs. The sensation was a thousand times stronger, more arousing and enticing than she could ever imagine—as though she could feel every cell of her skin as he brushed his fingers over it. Her eyes tracked his as he studied her seriously.

"You can hate us," said Connor. "But know that we love you and we chose to keep you here. You were meant to be ours, not to sleep in the company of angels."

His words struck something bittersweet inside her. A strange dream of an angel with wings of diamonds and fire… She blinked away fresh tears. Her father's voice echoed in her mind. *"Your place is back there, with them."*

When had he said that? She couldn't seem to recall. Funny, she felt as though she was missing something, but whatever it was, it didn't matter anymore. She flung her arms around Connor's neck, covering his face with kisses. Then she turned and opened her arms to Ian. He scooped her up, pulling her toward him as he took her mouth hungrily, his lips trembling beneath hers. When they pulled apart, she was laughing.

Ian's brows rose. "Well, that certainly was not the reaction we expected."

Connor chuckled darkly. "It certainly wasn't the way I acted when I was turned."

"Me neither. Then again, our sire had not exactly been the welcoming sort." Ian nuzzled her cheek, his long lashes tickled her newly sensitive skin.

Zoey pulled back and looked at them both. "Is it hard? Being a vampire?"

"It won't be easy. At first you'll fight hunger for blood every day, but we can help you. We'll teach you everything you need to know. How to feed and not kill. How to control the glamour."

"And I can stay…" She was afraid to ask more clearly what she wanted to know.

"With us. Forever." Ian stroked her back soothingly.

"That's all I've ever wanted," she whispered. "The only present I could have hoped for."

Ian winked at her. "Better than the flannel PJs?"

"The PJs are a close second."

She leaned into Ian and Connor hugged her from behind, the embrace warming her body and her soul. She wasn't alone, and she'd never be alone again.

A new chapter had opened for her, and she couldn't wait to see how this new life would unfold.

THANKS FOR READING THE BITE of Winter. I hope you enjoyed it! Keep Reading below for a free book offer, and a three chapter preview of one of my favorite stories involving a sexy, brooding hero, a curse, and a haunted castle!

Want a free romance novel? Fill out the form at the bottom of this link and you'll get an email from me with details to collect your free read!

Claim your **FREE** book now at:

www.laurensmithbooks.com/free-books-and-newsletter/

Find Me:

Twitter : **@LSmithAuthor**

Facebook : **www.facebook.com/LaurenDianaSmith**

I share upcoming book news, snippets and cover reveals plus PRIZES! Reviews help other readers find books. I appreciate all reviews, whether positive or negative. If one of my books spoke to you, please share! You've just read the first book in the Love Bites series. There will be more adventures and passionate love stories soon to come in this series!

———◆———

Want to read the first chapter of ANY of my books to see if you like it? Check out my Wattpad.com page where I post the first chapter of every book including ones not yet released!

To start reading visit:

www.wattpad.com/user/LaurenSmithAuthor

If you'd like to read the first three chapters from

THE SHADOWS
OF
STORMCLYFF HALL

the first book in the DARK SEDUCTIONS SERIES,
please turn the page.

PROLOGUE

Weymouth, England, 1811

THE CRASH OF THUNDER WOKE Richard, Earl of Weymouth. The fire in the hearth was low, the embers no longer crackling, and a cold draft pressed in around him as a storm raged outside. Pulling a loose sheet around his hips, he reached across the bed for his wife, who was still weak from bearing him a healthy son a month ago. His hands stopped short as he encountered nothing but the twisted sheets where her body had lain.

An icy tendril of fear churned in his stomach. She never left their bed when it rained. Storms frightened her. Isabelle usually curled into his side, burying her face against his throat for comfort.

Heavy rain whipped against the windows, the fierce staccato a warning to stay inside. Wind whistled through the room, teasing tapestries out, then back against the walls as though bodies moved behind them. A rumble of thunder seemed to shake the stones of his ancestral home, Stormclyffe Hall.

"Isabelle?" he called out. "Love?"

Only the crash of thunder answered.

Lightning streaked past the window and illuminated his son's cradle.

A sharp cry split the air.

Richard leapt out of bed, the icy floor stinging his bare feet as he rushed to the cradle. Murmuring soft, sweet words, he lifted his son, Edward, tucking him in the crook of one arm, relieved the babe was safe. He never thought he would be the paternal sort, but Isabelle and their babe brought out the tenderness in him.

The town viewed his marriage as a disgrace. Earls didn't marry the daughters of innkeepers. But Richard hadn't cared. He loved her and would do anything to have her in his life.

A frown tugged down the corners of his lips. "Where is your mother, Edward?"

Thunder once again rocked the hall. October storms thrashed the castle and nearby cliffs with a wicked vengeance. Trees were split in half by lightning; the edges of the cliff decayed inward, inching ever closer to the castle. Although the storm this night was no different, something felt wrong. A bite to the air, a sense of dread digging into his spine.

As the baby's long eyelashes drowsily settled back on his plump cheeks, Richard assured himself that the baby's linens were dry and Edward was content. He brushed his lips over his son's forehead and set him back in the cradle.

When he stepped back, glancing out the window that overlooked the sea, his blood froze. A feminine silhouette clambered through the rock outcroppings by the cliff's edge.

Even from a distance, he knew with a horrifying certainty it was Isabelle.

It was madness to be outside, alone by the cliffs. She knew the dangers, knew the soft dirt around the cliffs crumbled into the sea. Only the year before, a boy from the village had fallen to his death when the ground by the edge gave way.

"Isabelle!" he breathed, the single intake of air burning his chest as though fire had erupted within.

Before he had time to move, the sky blackened, his vision robbed of light.

When lightning again bathed the rocks, Isabelle was gone.

His stomach clenched with a fear so profound, it flayed open his chest with poison-tipped claws.

Shouting for his cloak and boots, he raced from the room. The nurse emerged from down the hall, her white cap askew, and gray hair frizzing out from under the edges.

"Take charge of the baby!" he yelled as he ran past her.

She nodded and hurried to his room.

His valet, followed by several footmen, raced to his aid, carrying clothes. He snatched them and dressed as he ran, his men right behind him dashing through the deluge.

When they reached the cliffs, there was no sign of Isabelle.

"My lord!" a footman by the edge shouted.

Afraid to look, yet unable to tear his eyes away, Richard stared down to where the man's finger pointed. The black shadow of Isabelle's cloak caught on a razor-thin piece of rock, fluttering madly like a bat's wing. Lightning slashed above them, its terrible light revealing a dark smear beneath the cloak's erratic movements.

Blood. Isabelle's blood. Had she jumped to her death?

"No!" A crash of thunder swallowed his roar of despair.

He dove for the edge, wanting to follow her into the frothing gray seas. A cloak smeared with blood. All that remained of his wife.

He'd fought too hard to win her love, her trust. They'd suffered through too much together, to be divided now. He couldn't raise Edward alone.

"No…please, no." The pleading came from the bottom of his soul, torn from his heart.

She was gone.

Strong arms hauled Richard back from the ledge, pinning him to the earth.

"It is too late, my lord. She's gone."

She was his Isabelle, his heart…

Why had she jumped? Had she been unhappy? It couldn't be that. He would have known, and he would have done everything in his power to make her happy.

"We must find her," he told the men standing around him.

An older man, Richard's head gardener, shook his head. "We

can't search in this weather, and her body will be gone by the time the storm ends. But we'll try to find what we can on the morrow, if you wish."

"I do," Richard growled. Despair was replaced with vengeance.

He faced Stormclyffe. Lightning laced the skies behind it in a white, delicate pattern. The centuries-old castle loomed out of the darkness, a defensive wolf with the battlements as its bared teeth.

It didn't matter that his infant son waited in a lonely cradle, eager for the loving touch of his remaining parent.

Richard was lost.

He wanted nothing to do with the life he'd had, the riches, the earldom. He despised it all. Every blessed memory he ever had that reminded him of Isabelle made him furious. She was gone from his life forever. He could not bring himself to dwell on his son; it only cleaved his chest in two. His love, his heart, was being battered against the rocks below.

CHAPTER 1

Weymouth, England, Present Day

BLOOD SPLASHED AGAINST WHITE PORCELAIN, the ruby red liquid spreading outwards in a chaotic pattern.

Jane Seyton hissed, clutching her leg. The cut burned like the devil. She slapped a palm over the sliced flesh, but crimson liquid seeped through her fingers. She set down her razor and reached for the shower nozzle, aiming it at the red streaks, washing it down the drain. A thin trail of red still trickled down the tub's edge, and she blasted with the nozzle again, desperately trying to erase the unsettling sight of her own blood.

She hobbled out of the shower, rummaging through her make-up bag until she found a Band-Aid.

Her room in the tiny inn was quiet, the silence thick and a little unsettling. She hummed to break up the suffocating lack of noise.

It had been a tiring journey from Cambridge to the small, desolate coast near Weymouth in Southern England. The White Lady Inn had an almost macabre wooden sign, a silhouetted woman in white standing at the edge of a vast cliff side, her dress billowing out to sea in a cloud of smoke-like swirls. It swung above the door and creaked with the slightest breeze. Despite the inn being situated between a lively pub and a quaint grocery store, there seemed to be a zone of quiet within the inn itself. Her room was a drab little place, with a narrow bed and whitewashed walls.

The same family had owned this inn for over two hundred years, passing it down from generation to generation. It was only natural that the place had seen better days and could use a little work. Yet, the awful silence made her skin tingle. She'd hardly slept last night, jumping at every small creak and groan. Taking herself to task, she'd consciously reminded herself that older places made such noises as the wood and stone settled into place.

Today she was driving up to the old castle-like manor house, Stormclyffe Hall, where she was going to meet the owner, the ninth Earl of Weymouth. After several emails back and forth, he'd reluctantly given her permission to tour the grounds along with other visitors but made no mention of getting access to the house's historical papers. Her dissertation was on the tragic stories of some of Britain's ancient castles and manor houses and with a particular emphasis on Stormclyffe and its affect on Weymouth. Her committee chair, Dr. Blackwell, had given her two weeks to find sources to supplement her theories on Stormclyffe Hall. Since the last four years of research footwork had been done towards this one particular castle, she couldn't switch the focus easily to another location. If she couldn't get what she needed, she wouldn't get Blackwell's approval and she'd have to start her dissertation—for a Ph.D. in history—over completely.

In order to complete her research, she had to find out what actually happened to the current earl's ancestors, Richard and his wife, Isabella, who'd both died under mysterious circumstances. Rumor had it Isabella had committed suicide. People claimed to have seen her ghost walking the cliffs. Richard had been found one foggy morning shortly thereafter sprawled in his study, a broken brandy glass next to his body. He had apparently drunk himself to an early grave a year after his wife's passing. The locals claimed the earl's spirit was trapped within the walls of his castle, restlessly searching for his dead wife, his mournful cries piercing the air on windless nights.

What Jane hadn't told the current earl or anyone else was the more personal reason for her focus on Stormclyffe Hall. Ever since she'd seen an old photo of it, she felt an almost mystical pull.

Lately she couldn't seem to focus on anything else.

The hall whispered to her on the darkest of nights, with soft murmurs and teasing visions just as she began to fall asleep. Before dawn, she'd awaken, hands trembling with the feel of heavy stones against her palms, her heart racing and lips drawn back in a scream as though she'd fallen from the cliffs herself. What she felt, however, in each and every dream she had lately were hands shoving at her lower back, pushing her over the edge against her will.

The obsession with Stormclyffe had cost her so much already. The months of work on her dissertation were now at risk of being set aside if she couldn't find primary sources. It would be back to square one if she had to pick another castle and start all of her initial research over again, but that wasn't the worst of it. Her fiancé Tim had broken off their engagement and ended their two-year relationship, telling her he found her obsession with the castle "creepy" and that he worried she was mentally unstable.

But Jane's dreams made her wonder if young countess hadn't jumped but been pushed by…someone. And that was the root of her obsession. The nightmares were slowly driving her mad, and she knew she had to get to the bottom of what happened to Isabella if she ever hoped to find peace. Because she wasn't sure how much longer she could stand waking up every night gasping for breath and her bones aching as though they'd smashed upon saltwater covered rocks. The last few months she and Tim had been together, her dreams had grown increasingly vivid and terrifying, and they'd woken him up as well.

The beginning of the end.

She would never forget the look on his face, the tightness to his eyes and the way his lips pursed as he'd held out his hand and asked for his engagement ring back. His bags were packed and sitting by the door, and he'd left within minutes of destroying her life and all of her hopes for the future. *Their future.*

With a little sigh, she smoothed her left thumb over the base of her naked fourth finger. Even after four months, she still felt bare without it. A splinter of pain shot through her chest, and she clenched her fist, avoiding looking at her hand anymore. She rubbed a towel through her hair before blow-drying it. She could have used a flat iron to tame the mess of dark waves, but she'd fried that when she first arrived in England and plugged it into the wall socket with a converter that hadn't worked properly. She'd never gotten around to buying another one.

Not that it mattered. Given that her academic pursuits tended to involve panels of older, balding male professors in tweed jackets, she rarely bothered with her looks. Her current mission, though, required a more professional touch to her hair and wardrobe. She figured if she looked fashionable and presentable, it might help further her research goals. Easier said than done. She was fully aware she wasn't the sort of woman men fawned over, but her dissertation depended on access to the earl's family archives, and she'd get dolled up if it would help make sure he didn't change his mind about letting her pry into his papers.

The current earl had proved initially reluctant to allow her access to his family history, but when she'd persisted through a deluge of emails and letters, he'd reluctantly said she'd be welcome to tour the grounds along with other tourists once the remodeling was over. That had been four months ago. Stormclyffe didn't have a website to clue her in on whether the grounds were open to tourists or not, but the remodeling had to be done by now. She couldn't wait any longer. And she wasn't going to take no for an answer on getting into those original sources from the current earl.

A smile tugged at her lips.

Sebastian Carlisle, the ninth Earl of Weymouth. A rich playboy with the world at his fingertips. Of course he was tall, with gorgeous, dark blond hair like melted gold and eyes the shade of cinnamon. By all reports, his life consisted of fast cars, leggy models with perfect hair, and wealth beyond imagining. The man was definitely not her type, but she needed to impress him if she was to stay at the castle and work.

Her Internet searches also revealed a fair amount about him, aside from his romantic entanglements, and she'd been impressed. With a PhD in history from Cambridge and degrees in numerous foreign languages, he showed a surprising amount of scholarship. Despite his flashy lifestyle, he'd helped push for preservation of historical landmarks throughout Britain and was a member of the Royal Historical Society.

His townhouse in London was rumored to have one of the country's best library collections, second only to other collections in aristocratic homes like Althorp, home to the ninth Earl Spencer. Even she had to admit that despite Carlyle's reputation as the most seductive man in all of England, he may also be one of the smartest.

She slipped into her favorite pair of jeans and a comfortable pair of black boots before donning a thick, gray, cable-knit sweater. Back home in Charleston, the weather would be light and warm, but the English coast was always cold in late October. Sea spray drifted far into town, sinking into her bones through the walls of the White Lady Inn.

Though it was still early afternoon, the sky outside her room dimmed as the low-hanging clouds drifted off the sea, dragging their vast looming shapes through the town and blocking out the sun's illumination. A chill seeped through the glass of the window, frosting the edges with dew that pebbled around the panes.

A sudden knot gathered at the base of her skull, the tiny hairs on the back of her neck rising. The air inside was now as cold as outside. Her breath exhaled in a cottony puff, and her skin tingled with a strange sensation. Her muscles tensed in response as though her body expected something to happen. If she hadn't known without a doubt that she was alone, she would have sworn someone was watching her.

She pushed the unsettling thought aside and retrieved her briefcase and purse. Tucked safely inside were her notebook and the latest letter she'd received last week from Sebastian Carlisle. She'd memorized every word.

Dear Ms. Seyton,
Thank you for your interest and inquiry into the Carlisle
ancestral home, Stormclyffe Hall. As its caretaker and heir, I am

*very pleased that my ancestry has found merit in the esteemed
Cambridge halls from where you write.*

*Your dissertation subject is a very interesting one, and I do see
how it might benefit your study to have access to my family's
documents, and I would welcome your educated account of my
home. However, I am currently overseeing the restoration of
Stormclyffe, which includes the preservation of those documents
which you seek, and having a scholar under the roof while that
roof is being mended might prove distracting for both you and
the restoration staff. You are more than welcome to visit once
the restorations have been thoroughly completed. However, any
access to personal and private papers and documents that are
the property of my family are not open for public viewing. Weymouth has an excellent library with plenty of sources you might
consider as an alternative avenue for research.*

*Please feel free to contact me, or the office of my steward Mr.
John Knowles, in the future should you have any other ques-
tions.*
Sincerely,
Weymouth

Jane's heart skittered. *Weymouth.* He hadn't even bothered to
sign his usual title "Earl of Weymouth." Just *Weymouth*. It rolled
off the tongue so nicely.

To think it had taken half a dozen letters to his office and more
than thirty emails to finally get his attention. His reply letter had
been very British, polite and yet firm. It was obvious he didn't
want her to come, at least not in her capacity as a researcher, but
only as a tourist. *Ha!* He had no idea what he was in for. She was
going to get into those documents.

The drive to Stormclyffe was beyond breathtaking. Weymouth
was a charming harbor town, dotted with multicolored buildings
that faced the edge of the water inlets like merry greeters. The
forest of sailboat masts rose and fell as the sea rippled beneath

the boats, lifting and dropping them in an endless waltz that enchanted her as she drove past. It was a place she could see herself living in for the rest of her life. She loved the idea of the cozy little place nestled next to the vast acreage of the Weymouth estate. She looked forward to leaving Stormclyffe on little breaks to pop down to the city and eat at the local pubs or visit the little shops and historical sites.

She drove past Weymouth Beach. The jubilee clock at the edge of the parking lot separated the beach from the shops and businesses. Its blue and red painted tower held the clock aloft for the residents to see the time at a distance. It painted a beautiful image, the clock at the edge of the shore, facing both sea and village. It stood as a silent sentinel over the flock of tourists that frolicked on the sand and in the shallows.

The twenty-minute drive to the estate took her on a narrow road that paralleled the edge of the coast. Although it was October, the grass was still green on the hillsides, and storm clouds were only a vague outline on the horizon. The landscape gave way to a slowly rising hill, and a mass of distant trees, gnarled and knotted together tight as thorns. Just beyond was a glimpse of the castle. It was a massive edifice that stood stark against the sky and trees, towering over the fields, and she couldn't help but stare.

The countless photographs she'd collected over the years hadn't prepared her for the raw beauty and power of the structure. The worn battlements were still fully intact, facing the sea like warriors, ever defiant in the face of nature's force on the coast. The steep cliffs merely a half a mile from the castle loomed, dark and threatening.

No fence lined the cliff edges. No warning signs guided visitors away except one that read *"Private Property. Heavy Fines for Trespassing."* She repressed an achy shiver as a cloud stole across the sun's path, dimming all light.

The gray stones of Stormclyffe stood stalwart and proud, challenging her to drive closer. The road turned to gravel and thinned even more, leaving only enough space for her car.

Sheer desolation seemed to pour off the structure as she pulled into the castle's front drive. If not for the five work vehicles that obviously belonged to various handymen, she would have thought the castle was devoid of all life.

Strands of hair stung her face as the wind whipped it about. There was an unsettling silence on the grounds, like something unnatural muffled the sound of the sea. No crashing waves, only the violence of the wind against the castle's stones.

The house seemed to be wrapped in an invisible layer of thick wool, where sight and smell was dulled. The wind's icy fingers crawled along her shoulder blades and dug into her hair, making her tense with apprehension. The castle walls were pitted with small chinks in the stones like fathomless obsidian eyes that stared at her, sized her up, and found her wanting.

The hairs rose on the back of her neck. The eerie sensation of eyes fixed on her back sent a cold wave of apprehension over her skin. She whipped around to look at the deserted landscape, suddenly fighting off a rush of panic at being alone out here.

Her heartbeat froze for a brief moment. A woman in a long white nightgown, hair loose down to her waist, stood hesitantly on the cliff's edge, half turned towards the sea. She stared at Jane. Her skin was grayish, and her eyes were shadowed with black circles as though she hadn't slept in years. Something wasn't right about the way she looked, or the fact that the nightgown looked far too old in style for any modern woman to be wearing. Not to mention a woman in a nightgown in broad daylight wasn't right either…

Sadness filled Jane's chest, choking her. It was as if she were infused with the same lonely desperation evident on the woman's face. Surprisingly, Jane felt no fear, merely the overwhelming grief that had come the moment she locked eyes with the woman. As though pulled by an unseen force, she took a step in the woman's direction. The skies above darkened to a black thunderous storm on the verge of breaking. Before she could get any closer, black roots burst forth from the rocks below the woman's slippered feet, winding up her calves and digging into her skin like thorns.

Jane had no time to react—her breath caught in her throat as the woman's eyes widened. Jane struggled to move, but her body wouldn't obey. Every muscle was tensed and yet frozen like stone. The woman opened her mouth, a silent scream ricocheting off the insides of Jane's skull. Then the thorny roots pulled her off the edge of the cliffs and into the sea.

"No!" A gasp escaped Jane's lips, barely above a whisper. Her skin broke out in goosebumps, and she shook her head, trying to clear it of what she'd just seen. Her hand shot to clutch her necklace, a pendant gifted to her by her grandmother.

Before she could even run to the edge, a voice cut through her shock. "She isn't real. Just a phantom." The quiet voice intruded on her terror.

She glanced over her shoulder. A handsome man in his mid-thirties dressed as a gardener approached, carrying a pair of huge shears. The sight was so unexpected after what she'd just witnessed that she wasn't quite sure how to react. Brown eyes studied her with a mixture of pity and concern.

"What did you say?"

The man sighed, set his shears down, leaning them against his knee while he rubbed his palms on his brown work pants. "What you saw there, was the lady in white. She's haunted these cliffs since her death."

Her death? The woman she'd just seen was a…ghost?

"You believe in ghosts?" Jane turned her face once more to the cliffs.

The gardener turned his head towards the sea, his eyes focusing on something from the past. "I believe that evil leaves its mark on a place. Burns itself in the stones so deep that only something truly pure and good can get it out. These old stones have so much evil buried in them, I doubt the castle will ever rest. It isn't safe here, not for you." The gardener bent to pick up his shears again. "You should go, return to wherever you've come from, and forget this place."

She swallowed, a metallic taste still thick in her throat, focusing back on the gardener. "How often have you seen her? The lady in white?" Even as she spoke, the image of the woman's face flashed across her mind, and a chill swept through her entire body. She rubbed her hands over her arms.

He shrugged, eyes facing the cliffs as he answered. "She appears there on the cliffs whenever her kin return home."

She looked towards the hall, trying to bury the memory of sorrow and fear on the ghost's face. Anyone else might have been panicking after having just seen what she'd seen. But the nightly visions plaguing her had slowly forced her to accept that there were things beyond her explanation. Like ghosts.

"So the earl is here?" The earl was in residence. This was good news. She had been a little worried that he may be monitoring the estate from London.

"Yes. Arrived seven months ago. Been trying to restore the place. Not much good will it do. The ghosts are stirring again. He's upset the balance."

"The balance?" A sense of warning niggled at the back of her head, but she forced herself to ignore it—and to ignore the sense that she was losing her mind.

The gardener appeared to really see her for the first time. "The balance. Between the evil and the good. Evil rules the castle. Stalks the halls and torments those who dare to live inside."

Icy fingers raked down Jane's back.

"Is Lord Weymouth in danger? Being in the house?" It only occurred to her after she asked that the gardener might be right, and *she* might be in danger too.

The gardener looked out to sea, his eyes dark. "I don't know. But if you plan to stay here, watch yourself, miss. Evil isn't always what you'd expect. It can take many forms." His voice dropped. "Many forms."

He turned and walked away. The momentary comfort his presence provided her vanished as she gazed upon his retreating form.

She wanted to know what he meant, but she doubted she'd get much more from him. She turned her attention back to the castle. The high windows reflected the sunlight as it started to peek out from the clouds.

The image of the lady in white flashed through her mind again, blinding her to the present for a brief instant. Her heart clenched in sadness, and fear rippled through her in tiny little waves, enough to keep her on edge. Had she witnessed a true apparition, or had her own imagination run away with her? She'd half-hoped her dreams of being pushed from the cliffs had been only nightmares, yet that woman looked so familiar..

She had always believed in supernatural things. She was no longer a practicing Catholic in the church-going sense, but her faith was strong enough that she respected the truth that there were things in this world she couldn't understand. Like ghosts. And now she was going to enter a place bleeding with evil. She reached up to clutch the medallion of the archangel Michael that hung around her neck. The metal was warm from lying against her skin. It was a small comfort in the face of the looming castle and the fears of what might lurk in its shadows.

CHAPTER 2

HE WAS CURSED. THERE WAS no other explanation for it. Bastian Weymouth glared at the expensive toilet in his bathroom. Arms crossed over his chest, he shot a glance at the portly plumber who quivered in the doorway.

"What has you so agitated? I see nothing wrong." Bastian studied the room again, searching for signs of the disaster that the plumber insisted had taken place just a few minutes before he'd run to find Bastian.

The plumber gulped and took a deep breath. "The toilet was in place, and I was just tightening the pipes when the water exploded out of the bowl. It flooded the whole room!" The plumber waived his wrench about.

Bastian's displeasure deepened. The room wasn't wet. There wasn't one drop of water outside the bowl to confirm the plumber's story.

"I swear on my life, my lord! Water up to my ankles." The plumber jabbed at his pants where it showed the fabric soaked clear through up to his calves.

Yet the entire room was completely dry, and the plumber had only fetched him a moment ago to explain the flooding. Flooding, which by all appearances, hadn't ever occurred.

It was just one more irritation in a long line of complications that had occurred during the renovations, begun when he'd moved back to Weymouth and Stormclyffe seven months ago, after his family's fifty-year absence. Leaky roofs, window panes shattering just hours after being installed, birds finding their way inside and dying when they broke their necks against the walls trying to escape. There were even workers talking about seeing a woman in a white dress along the cliffs. He'd never seen anything like that here. It was utter nonsense, but the list went on from there, each thing more frustrating than the last. All of it worsened the superstitions of the locals, especially the ones he had hired to repair everything. If he could just get the repairs completed, all of the superstitious nonsense would have to stop. The mutterings of "cursed" as he walked past local shops in the town would have to stop, too. He was tired of the black label his family bore in Weymouth because of the tragedies in their ancestral past. Restoring Stormclyffe, fixing it was the key. Something deep inside him compelled him to save the Hall. It was an almost tangible need to see the broken glass panes of the windows mended, and the rooms dusted, the broken stones replaced. Maybe returning the Hall to its former glory would make it look less like a tourist attraction for ghost hunters, and would make the townspeople stop spreading tales about it Then he might have a chance at a somewhat normal life, rather than be the target of village gossip.

And his grandmother had been convinced that if he could fix the Stormclyffe, there would be no more problems, no more tragedies, no more lost loved ones, like his father.

"It is fine, Mr. Tibbs. I'll compensate you for your services. I trust you'll stay here to see to the remaining water closets?"

"Thank you, my lord, but I have to say I don't feel comfortable staying here after dusk." The portly man shifted on his feet, eyes darting around the lavish bathroom. "I'll return first thing in the morning."

Bastian didn't blame him. It was obvious Tibbs was a superstitious sort, and given the bloody history of Stormclyffe…well, that wasn't a surprise. Bastian's newly married grandparents had fled the castle in 1962 after an upstairs maid was found hanging from the rafters of the great hall. And they hadn't been the first to leave over the Hall's last two centuries.

The authorities hadn't been able to figure out how the girl

had gotten out to the center beam to hang herself; there was no way it could be reached without an impossibly tall ladder. Yet the maid had been discovered swinging all the same. Nessy Harper, the victim, had been a local girl, and his family's reputation with the nearby town had been blackened. The coroner's report had read suicide, but there had been talk about his grandfather driving Nessy to it in some sort of doomed love affair. Bastian knew it was nonsense, but it didn't make the sting to his family's honor and pride any less significant.

Bastian's grandmother, who'd spent her last days in their London townhouse, had died murmuring about Nessy. He grimaced at the memory of her last moments when he'd been alone with her.

"Beware the shadows Bastian…they hold evil. Stay away from the castle. Poor sweet Nessy, milk-white eyes…she was so scared… Touch not the heart of evil… What once was broken must be mended." The frail old woman exhaled, and six-year-old Bastian had screamed. Her words had never made sense, but he'd always wondered if she'd meant that the castle shouldn't lay empty and crumbling. His grandparents had been the last heirs to live in the castle after all, and the guilt of leaving it behind might have weighed upon her in her final hours. Many people suffered from delusions and superstitions in their twilight years.

"Tibbs, I'll pay triple your price if you get this toilet up and running before sunset."

The plumber's eyes bugged out in surprise. He nodded and rushed off to collect more tools.

Bastian left the water closet and headed back downstairs, ignoring the chaos of repair people and staff he'd hired to help with the upkeep of the castle.

"My lord," his butler, Randolph, announced. "The stone mason has finished repairing his work on the bell tower, but he said to advise you that if you wish to have the bell working properly you'll need to replace the clappers since all of the bells are missing them."

"Fine. I'll add it to the list of things I need to fix."

When Bastian turned to leave, his butler coughed politely. "One more thing, my lord. You have a visitor. I put her in the red drawing room."

Bastian cocked an eyebrow and scowled. "A visitor?" That was the last thing he needed.

Randolph swallowed, his eyes shifting away. "Er, yes. She said she is here to do research on the house, and you invited her in a letter. She's American."

American? For a second he couldn't imagine who Randolph was talking about. When the butler handed him the letter in question, obviously taken from the visitor, he studied it.

"Er…Yes. I remember." He scanned the note he'd hastily written several months ago. It all came back, the numerous emails and phone calls from the American woman named Jane Seyton. He'd asked her to wait until renovations were complete before she visited, yet here she was, showing up in the middle of numerous disasters. He'd made it abundantly clear she wasn't allowed any access to his family's archives. Apparently Americans didn't understand blunt honesty. No surprise. He crumpled the letter in his fist, failing to quell the sudden frustration.

As if superstitious workmen weren't enough to cause him trouble, having the American here would prove to be one more irritation. She would have to be supervised to make sure she didn't pry into his family's documents and that nothing was taken intentionally from the house.

Randolph cleared his throat. "Will she be staying here, my lord? I can have a room prepared immediately."

Stay here? Surely he couldn't let the woman stay in the castle. Bastian was about to declare as much when something out of the corner of his eye flickered. A shadow at the edge of his vision seemed to be creeping along the wall towards him. He turned and focused in the direction he'd glimpsed it, but all signs of the shadow were gone.

I'm seeing things too, blast it! These workmen are driving me to madness as well. He rubbed his eyes with his thumb and forefinger.

"My lord?" Randolph prompted, which made Bastian realize

he must have been silent for several moments. The shadows had him on edge. Perhaps it would be nice to have a bit of company, if only she wasn't a bloody American. Given the rumors of ghosts and other such childish stories, most of the staff at Stormclyffe refused to stay overnight. Only Randolph and a few of the loyal staff from London remained after dark.

"I shall meet with her. She will not be staying here."

Jane Seyton was sure to be like every other historian he'd met and probably as stubborn as one of the Queen's corgis with a bone. Given half the chance, she'd run off to the nearest garden and bury his secrets where only she could find them. He didn't like anyone having that power over him.

Well, he did have a way with women. If she proved too troublesome in getting her to leave, he'd simply seduce her. There wasn't a woman born yet that would say no to an invitation to dinner if the Earl of Weymouth asked them. No doubt she was a lonely little bookworm, probably wearing spectacles and never been kissed. The idea was almost charming. He smirked as he headed towards the drawing room. If he wanted her gone by nightfall, she'd be gone and all it would cost him was dinner.

When he reached the drawing room and laid a palm on the heavy oak door, it swung open revealing the rich red- and gold-papered walls and covered furniture. He hadn't had the chance to visit every room in the castle in the last seven months, since he'd been here sparingly, and he had definitely not been into this one. Randolph had been overseeing the cleanup of the rooms upon Bastian's instructions and given the number of rooms, many had yet to be opened.

Personally, he had been avoiding this room, because it was the only one in the castle where a portrait of Isabelle hung. His grandmother had said looking upon Isabelle's face was bad luck, and since Stormclyffe had been abandoned for longer than he'd been alive, he'd never had the chance to find out himself it was true. But now, seeing his ancestor for the first time…he was arrested at the sight.

There on the wall was the infamous woman whose swan dive

off the cliffs had tainted his family's lives forever. Bastian studied the portrait for a moment. A fair-skinned woman with a hint of rose in her cheeks gazed out from the layers of oil with serious gray eyes. Her pale blue gown molded to her curves, and waves of rich ebony hair tumbled down her shoulders to tease the tops of her breasts. There was a curious expression on her face. She was happy, but wariness lurked in the depths of her eyes, as though she expected to lose her joy at any moment.

Below the painting, a flesh-and-blood woman stood with her back to him. Windblown hair, dark as a raven's wing, spiraled down her back in enticing waves. He had the sudden urge to thread his fingers through the silken strands and shape her full curves with his other hand. A curious burning settled deep in his bones, and a ringing filled his ears as visions of him pinning her to a bed filled his mind. Wild, erotic thoughts tumbled through him, stealing his breath before he regained control and focused on his visitor again.

As though she'd heard his lustful thoughts, the woman turned to face him, cheeks flaming. She couldn't have known what he was thinking. His hand dropped from the door handle, his jaw slackened in shock.

The dreamy gray eyes fixed on him were identical to the eyes of the woman painted above her. Noble, high cheek bones, curving brows, a sensual mouth made for kisses, and that nose, both delicate and impish, a perfect fit for the face of the woman before him. Her inky black tresses and curves designed perfectly for a man's hands made her a living memory of a woman centuries gone.

Dear God… He repeated the words in his head over and over, mesmerized by the closeness of their shared features.

"You must be Lord Weymouth. I'm Jane Seyton."

The woman strode over to him, hand outstretched. Without thinking, he took it. Heat flared between them. He inhaled sharply.

She dropped his hand and retreated a step, her eyes wide. Had she felt the same jolt he had?

"I sent you a letter explaining that there couldn't be visitors here until renovations were complete. I also told you that I wouldn't let you see any of my family's documents." He grunted, but his gaze kept straying to the portrait behind her, comparing her features to Isabelle's. There was no obvious difference, and that alone had him blinking.

"I waited four months. I assumed the renovations were complete..." Her gaze darted around the room, and she seemed to hesitate as though mentally kicking herself for believing the work would be done so soon. "If you'd only let me see the documents, I could be out of here in a week at most, I swear. I just need enough to be able to write a publishable thesis."

For some reason, her reaction angered him. He didn't want her here when the castle wasn't looking as it should. It was a reflection of him and his family, and to have her intrude was strange, even unsettling. A rush of temper overcame him—one he didn't know he could possess. The powerful emotion was almost foreign, as though not entirely his own.

"Are all of you Americans like this? Barge into a man's home, seeking evidence of scandals that ruined his family for two centuries? Have you no thought to how that destroys my family's fragile reputation?" he growled low through clenched teeth.

Her lips thinned, and the color in her cheeks faded. She looked pale, vulnerable, as though his outburst had upset her.

Her lovely eyes disappeared from his view as her gaze dropped to the floor. "I'm so sorry. I didn't realize it would be such an inconvenience." She sounded genuinely apologetic.

With a heavy sigh, he let his tense shoulders drop. "I apologize for my harsh reply, Miss Seyton. But really, you must leave. I am having trouble with the workmen, and we keep running into problems."

Her face brightened, gray eyes sparkling with energy again. "I need this, Lord Weymouth. If I can't find primary sources to accompany my assertions on the effect of the tragedies of Storm-clyffe on the Weymouth community, my committee chair won't approve of my paper, and I'd have to start over on a totally new topic. I wouldn't be in your way. I'll stick to the libraries, the attics. That sort of thing. I could help you, if you like. I'm handy at quite a few things, not just research."

An odd stirring deep in Bastian turned his irritation at her into something different so quickly he barely had time to acknowledge it.

Desire.

Caught in slow-building currents of fascination and hunger for this complete and total stranger, he wanted to see if her handiness extended to activities between the sheets. She seemed to glow with a repressed sexuality, a woman unaware of her appeal. This was not the bookish woman he'd expected. Whatever he'd envisioned she would be like, perhaps wearing a tweed dress suit, spectacles perched on her nose, and a prim chignon, she was certainly not that.

There was something natural about her that appealed to him. She wore no makeup, and she was lovelier for it. Her somewhat casual attire looked comfortable, yet sophisticated. Quite unlike any of the women he had dated in the past. She was a woman who wouldn't wear a slinky dress and strappy high heels. Her sensuality was the sort that would flower before him when he had her naked on a bed.

What an image that was!

It took every ounce of his willpower to convince his body that a physical response was not a good idea. He closed the door and leaned back against it, examining her face, trying desperately to focus on it and not the rest of her body.

"Why do you care so much about the history of this place? I know from your letters you've never been here before. Why Stormclyffe? Why the obsession over people who are dead and gone? You can't change the past." In that brief instant, Bastian wondered who he was trying to convince, himself or her. He didn't know.

She turned away, moving about the room. She paused to pick up a framed photograph of his grandparents. Dust from the shelf, disturbed by her movement, wove through the streaks of sunlight coming in from the windows.

"There's something about Stormclyffe. It calls to me." Another blush highlighted her face, accenting her lovely cheeks. "I want to learn everything about it and uncover its secrets. You have to let me stay. *Please*."

He snatched a photograph out of her hand, clutching it to his chest with one palm. "Ms. Seyton."

"Jane."

It disturbed him. He couldn't get a read on this woman, couldn't decide why she was so interested in his home. It was obvious that her desire to stay wasn't just out of a scholarly interest. There was something more there, but she wouldn't tell him…yet.

He set the photograph aside on a shelf above her reach.

"What secrets do you think lurk in my home, *Jane*?" His voice caressed her name, hoping his silky tone would crumble her defenses a little. He had to regain command of the situation.

She nibbled her bottom lip, and a wave of arousal slammed into him like a freight train. A thousand delicious thoughts flashed through his head of what he'd like to do to those lips. He practically had to shake his head to clear it of the growing lust. What was wrong with him? He'd never been so out of control before. No better than young man with his first girl, he couldn't keep his thoughts away from her and her body.

"Well?" He had the sudden desire to corner her, catch her, claim her. It had been ages since the predatory urge to seduce a woman had overtaken him. Bastian fought off his rising desire to unravel the puzzle she presented. Who was Jane Seyton? Sexy, yet innocent graduate student, or was she Mata Hari determined to seduce his secrets out of him for her own gain?

She pirouetted on her toe with all the grace of a ballerina and followed the line of bookshelves, one finger leaving a line in the dusty wood near the faded spines of the books.

"Jane," he growled and cornered her at the end of the left side of the drawing room.

"Hmm?" She spun to face him, eyes widening at him as he glared down at her. She was short, and he towered over her by a good eight inches.

His voice dropped from a growl to a husky whisper. "My family's history is an unhappy one, and it is crucial I maintain what little dignity the dead have left. I need to know why you want to dig up the past. And don't feed me any stories about your dissertation. I know there's another reason you are here."

When she opened her mouth to protest, he placed his finger over her lips. They weren't pouty or full like most women he considered beautiful, but rather were a pale pink and petal soft. Lust exploded through him, an inferno of heat and insanity a coiled whip, striking his body, screaming for release. Again that sense of being controlled, as though a foreign entity had taken him over. He continued to touch her mouth.

He rubbed his thumb over her bottom lip, imagining his tongue licking it before sliding inside. "I can't have you underfoot, writing your ghost stories, unless you can give me a bloody good reason to let you. And I *hate* ghost stories." He wanted to pin her against the wall and kiss her until she couldn't remember her name. The thought was so out of place, so unexpected.

How was it possible to know that if he were to kiss just beneath the delicate line of her jaw, she would purr like a kitten? Or if he were to rock his hips into hers that she would arch her back and demand a kiss so deep they both would be gasping for air? It should have worried him that he knew just what to do to please her, but he was too lost in this moment, this heady rush of need and fire for her.

Her eyes, like the turbulent seas, flashed in ire.

A pinprick of light just behind her head burst into view, glowing and pulsing like an icy heart. He tore his eyes from Jane's face and stared in shock at the light as it grew. His lips parted, but it shot straight at him before he could make a sound. The light engulfed him them and something rammed into him, rippled through his limbs, and took control.

He became a visitor in his own body, forced to watch from a distance, only feeling and seeing what the thing inside him wished him to experience. Fighting for a long moment against his loss of control, he finally surrendered, and the thing within took over fully, drawing him in, merging his consciousness with some unknown being.

"Isabelle!" A hoarse cry tore from his lips, yet the voice wasn't his.

There was no stopping it. A harsh passion seized him, and he pulled her body tight to his, pinning her wrists at her sides as he took her mouth. He trapped her between himself and the bookcase, reveling in her squeak of surprise.

In a frenzy, he explored her plush curves, his hands shaping and stroking every bit of her he could touch. It had been years, so many years since he'd touched her, his sweet Isabelle. She nipped his chin, her hands curling around his shoulders, digging in to drag him closer as she yielded to his dominance.

A roaring wind filled his ears, drowned out the thundering of his blood and the drumbeat of his heart. Glimpses between kisses revealed sharp electric blue spheres flaming like distant stars in the small black pupils of her eyes. She was there, beyond his reach, yet in his arms. How was this possible? He'd been trapped in the walls for nearly two centuries, unable to find her or hold her.

My beloved. Isabelle.

He groaned and released her wrists to cup her lush rounded bottom, lifting her against him, clenching hard as he rocked his aching cock against her heated center.

He rammed hard, driving himself against her, no matter that clothes separated him from his desire. She cried out against his ear, the sound a symphony of pleasure that snapped and cracked between them like flames devouring wood.

It was madness to want her, madness to need a stranger. He knew the body wasn't truly his Isabelle's but he could feel her inside it, trying to reach out to him.

But he did know her; something deep within him roared in defiance, as though his soul knew hers, even if his mind did not.

Must punish her. Must prove she cannot live without me.

"Why did you leave me? Why did you jump?" he demanded.

She shook her head, eyes wild and suddenly bright with fear.

He snarled against her lips and kissed her harder, one hand unbuttoning her trousers to loosen them, before sliding his hand beneath the waist of her pants to cup her arse. His fingers dipped between her thighs, finding wet heat. She moaned something unintelligible and shifted closer to him, urging him on with her body when words failed her. Her mouth met his with an equal fire and heady lust, just as she writhed against him, trying to satisfy her needs.

Surrender to me, love. Ease this ache of mine, my broken heart.

He tore his lips from hers and nibbled a path down her neck, savoring the faintly salty-sweet taste of her skin beneath his tongue.

His fingers stroked her entrance again and again until she shuddered and convulsed. He sank his teeth into her neck, hoping the love bite was hard enough to leave a mark so others would know she was his. For however long he possessed this body, for however long Isabelle was in his arms, he had to lay his claim to her. He pulled his hand out from between her thighs and wrapped his arms around her back, clutching her to him. How long would he have to hold her before he lost her again? He could feel his control of the body slipping…slipping away. Despair snuffed out his lust, and a chill surged through him. With a cry of rage and agony, he was torn from the body and forced back into the stones of Stormclyffe.

Freezing pain tore through Bastian, and his knees buckled. The foreign presence, that sense of someone else within him was gone. He went down like a stone, hitting the carpet. His eyelids fell shut. His breaths coming in soft pants were the only steady thing in him. The rest of him vibrated with energy, tiny electric shocks pulsing through his body.

After an eternity, the fog in his head seemed to clear. Every muscle in his body screamed in protest as he sat up. A body lay next to him, face down on the floor. A woman…the American. It all came rushing back. The passion, the fire, and the fact that he hadn't been in control of himself. He'd done things to her, possibly without her permission. And the name Isabelle still hung on his lips as though he had screamed it until he lost his voice.

What in God's name had happened? There was no rational explanation for what had just occurred. Knowing this made him shudder so harshly that his bones seemed to crack.

"Ms. Seyton—Jane…" He shook her awake.

She murmured groggily and rolled over onto her back.

"What the hell happened?" Her muttered curse was oddly reassuring. "Were we kissing?" She touched her kiss swollen lips and then her eyes flicked to his. "Oh my God. I swear I don't do this."

"I don't either…" he frowned and rubbed the back of his neck, trying to dispel the guilt at not being able to explain his actions. He'd kissed plenty of women, but never in such circumstances as these. It was as if he'd been…possessed. If such a thing could actually occur. Which it couldn't. "I'm sorry for whatever I might have…er… done to you without your consent."

He glanced down at his groin, worried at the sight of his erection. Why was his body not responding to his mind's wishes? There shouldn't be arousal, fire, passion. Yet all three of these were rioting through him making it perfectly clear his body still wanted to bed the woman sitting next to him. His gaze raked her, taking in the sight of her flushed cheeks, swollen lips…and teeth marks between her neck and shoulder.

"I remember going along with it and liking it, but I sort of felt like there was no control." She dragged her fingers through the tangle of black locks, and her gaze slid away, her cheeks pink as her fingers fumbled with the loose buttons of her jeans, securing them back in place.

Bastian felt like a damned fool. He'd just snogged a woman in his drawing room without any control over himself. If he were a man who believed in ghosts, he might think that his ancestor Richard had taken over his body. Possessed him. But that was *impossible*.

Bastian shrugged it off as nerves. He refused to let himself believe anything else. The castle renovations were getting to him. Maybe he was having some sort of psychotic breakdown from the stress.

Yes. That made sense. He was having a mental breakdown.

Jane got to her feet and held out a hand to him. He accepted, letting her pull him up and got a better look at her.

She wore jeans that hugged her shapely body and a thick gray sweater like she was ready to climb aboard his sailboat and float out on the tide with him. Again he was surprised that her natural beauty was such an allure to him. After years of polished, posh princesses, it was strange that a woman like this commanded his attention.

He was hardly a romantic. He'd never seen the need to fall in love or get involved in any messy entanglements of the heart. He took women, gave them pleasure, and sated his own needs. The romance of red roses and chocolates weren't for men like him. There was no need to buy appreciation from his women, nor did he particularly feel the need to reward them for succumbing to their passions in his arms. He preferred straining naked bodies in sweaty sheets to poetry and dinners for two. Sex was akin to business transactions, and although Bastian knew he viewed it coldly, he enjoyed it. He didn't need any of the emotional intimacy or love that many women seemed to think was required. And he'd never stopped to consider why that was.

But the idea of taking his time, savoring Jane's taste and inhaling the faint scent of her wild orchid perfume while he claimed her, was incredibly tempting.

"Why are you looking at me like that? Isn't it enough that you mauled me like a wild bear?" She shoved at him; her palm made contact with his chest, and he tensed with heat and need. Although upon first meeting her he expected her to be a timid little nose-in-her-book scholar type, she wasn't. Her politeness gave way to an intimacy that confused him. She wasn't exactly treating him the way others did, with respect and awe. No…she had just shoved him like she would a brother or perhaps a lover, or at the least someone she was comfortable with. Why had she done that?

Strangely, he realized her rough-and-tumble action fascinated him. Her sensual playfulness was incredibly erotic. None of the previous women he'd been with had ever been playful. They'd been coy and aggressive, but never teasing. He had to admit he liked it. A woman like her, with full curves and strength just ached to be taken hard, ravaged to within an inch of dying from too much pleasure.

He bit his lip so hard blood beaded, and he licked it away. If he didn't get inside Jane soon, pound into her sweet heat until she screamed he'd… Bastian wrenched control of his body back from that deep inner specter that seemed determined to pin her to the floor and spread her thighs. She was turning him inside out with desire. He hadn't wanted a woman this bad in a long time.

With every last ounce of willpower, he assumed the mantle of his British upbringing and scrounged deep down for the last bit of his manners. "I apologize profusely for my actions. I have no idea what came over me." And he meant it. How could he begin to explain what had just come over him?

She didn't reply, so he studied her for a long moment, those piercing eyes of hers cut straight through to his core. He couldn't help but wonder…she had kissed him back. She hadn't tried to push him away or fight him when he'd kissed her. Why?

"You have no idea why you kissed me?" Her tone sounded odd, as though she might know the answer to her own question.

He shrugged, completely at a loss to explain himself. "I haven't the slightest idea. I suppose it's all the stress from the renovations. I've had headaches for days now, and this is probably one more way my body is reacting. You see now why it's in your best interest to leave my house. I wouldn't want you to remain here when things could get…complicated." He placed a palm on the small of her back, ushering her to the door.

She twirled around, escaping his touch so she could go back and retrieve her briefcase and purse.

"Actually, I don't mind complicated. Perhaps my being here will help reduce the stress."

It took all of his control not to reply that the best de-stressing he could use was her on a bed beneath him.

"Miss Seyton, you cannot stay." He looped his arm through hers, attempting to drag her, albeit politely, towards the door.

She dug in her heels and wedged herself into the doorway. "Wait! Please! *What once was broken must be mended,*" her words were expelled in a breathless rush and he froze.

"What did you say?"

Her face darkened as she met his stare. "What once was broken must be mended."

"Where did you hear that?" He whirled her around, pinning her by her shoulders against the doorjamb.

"I…I don't know," she whispered. Her body trembled beneath his hands. "I can't explain it. It's like the words were on the tip of my tongue and when you tried to make me leave…they just rushed out."

His grandmother's warning. The need to fix his ancestral home. This woman who could be Isabelle's twin. It was as though puzzle pieces were sliding into place, but Bastian didn't want to see the puzzle. He didn't want to face this, whatever it was. He might lose more than he already had. Stormclyffe had taken his father, destroyed his grandfather's life, and countless other generations going back two hundred years. Anyone staying here was at risk. If Jane stayed she would be at risk, too.

"Let me stay. Please." Her begging undid the cold knot inside his chest.

Perhaps if he let her use the library, just for a short while, he could ply her with reasons the curse didn't exist and then send her on her way. If he was very lucky, he might stop her writing her thesis all together, so no one would come here in search of ghosts.

"If, and I do mean 'if,' I allow you to stay, you will not be permitted to review documents unless I have approved them first. You will go nowhere in this castle unless I have given express permission. I will give you one week. That is all. You will not disrupt me, nor the workmen, nor cause any kind of disturbance. Do you understand?"

She was already nodding eagerly before he'd even asked the last question.

A heavy sigh escaped his lips. "Very well. Then you may stay. But if at any point in time, I feel you are underfoot, I will have you leave, and you will brook no argument."

"Deal." She held out her hand.

He released his grip on her shoulders but didn't shake her hand.

Touching her once had led to violent passions. He would not be so foolish as to touch her again.

"Sorry," she muttered, dropping her hand.

For a moment they just stared at each other, neither of them speaking. He'd never felt so awkward in his life, but something about Jane ruffled his feathers.

She'd broken the spell of tension with a shrug and produced a notebook and pen, flipping to an empty page and started to scrawl notes. "So this has happened often?"

He purposely gave her a blank look, hoping it would dissuade her from further questions.

She continued. "The attempted seduction of visiting ladies?"

He rolled his eyes. What was he to do with this irritating and completely beguiling creature?

"Have you not been listening? There are no visiting ladies. You are the first official guest Stormclyffe has had in half a century. I only started renovations seven months ago and moved in a few months ago." He ushered her down a hallway, trying to remind himself where the library was. It would be a safe place to put her while he saw to his duties. No doubt she could lose herself in the books for hours, and he could check on her later. It would give him time to secure his more private papers in his office, away from her prying eyes. Even though he'd reluctantly agreed to let her stay, it didn't mean he had to provide her with any real substantial research material.

"So you didn't bring anyone with you? A girlfriend I mean?" Her blunt question caught him off guard, and he stumbled a step.

"What? No…I am not involved with anyone at the moment. I'm not one for getting involved at all really. In fact, I plan never to marry." Where that honesty came from, he didn't know, but he wanted her to hear it. Maybe that would make her understand what sort of man he was. One who didn't date women with designs on becoming the next Countess of Weymouth.

She raised a brow as they continued to walk down the long corridor. Much of the castle's exterior was stonework, but a good majority of the inside had been rebuilt to have a more modern design, well, modern enough at any rate. Bastian knew that most of the interior of the Hall was a combination of Regency and Georgian in style. Richard had been the last of his ancestors to make major changes to the architecture and design on the inside as well as select the furnishings.

She was still gazing at him somewhat reproachfully. "What's that look for?" he asked.

"Isn't there supposed to be an heir and a spare or something? You're an earl. Isn't that part of your heritage? Continue the family line and everything?"

He chuckled, the sound dark and almost unnatural, startling even himself. "I'm not sure my family line should be continued, given our history. Perhaps it's best if the line dies out with me."

She wrinkled her nose. "Then why fix the castle? Why bother if you don't plan to share the success of restoring your home with a family and making it last for generations to come."

"Damnation!" He halted and smacked a balled fist into his opposite palm. "Even if I'm the last, it doesn't mean what I'm doing is irrelevant. I don't plan to marry, but that doesn't mean I won't give my life purpose by rebuilding my family's ancestral home." Hadn't she herself whispered the words? *What once was broken must be mended?* The Hall was broken by grief, by tragedy, by loss. It wasn't just the stones, but if he started there, he might heal his family's wound. A meager hope, one he clung to without any real hope it would work. But what else could he do? Even if he never set foot in the Hall again, he feared the curse would cling to him and destroy anything he cared about. Better to be here alone and try to fix the place. He had to finish what his father started.

"I'm sorry. I didn't mean to offend you. I was just making an observation." She combed one hand through her hair, tugging it away from her face.

Bastian wasn't sure what he should have said in response to her apology and was grateful that the library door was a few feet away. After what had just happened, he needed some time to escape her and regain his composure and his control. The violent mood swings he had just experienced in the last few minutes were entirely unlike him, and he suspected her presence was at the root of their cause. Avoiding her at least temporarily might help him solve matters.

There wasn't much in the way of natural light in the castle, but Bastian's predecessors had installed modern lightning. A massive three-tiered chandelier hung in the great hall, crystals beading the cables that connected the tiers. The chandelier cast muted lights along the ceiling, the faint glow warming the room below. Cobwebs laced the corners of the halls, out of reach of even the most agile maids. The space between the rafters and the floor beneath their feet was filled with cold air.

"Bastian, this is where the maid died, right? In 1962?"

He froze, shoulders tensing, before he looked over at her. While the papers had published the news of the maid's mysterious death, no mention had been made nor pictures taken of the location of her body. How the bloody hell did this woman know where the maid had died? He raked a hand through his dark blond hair and scowled. "She was found hanging from the middle rafter." He pointed straight above them.

She craned her neck back, obviously considering the location of the beam. "How could she have gotten there? The beam isn't reachable from any place but the ground, and she would have needed a huge foot ladder. Don't you think it's odd?"

"It wasn't a suicide." His voice was harder than stone. "My family believes someone killed her."

She stilled, going so silent, it was as if she forgot to breathe.

"So who did it?" She caught up with him as he started walking again.

His gaze flicked to hers, a pulse of heat shooting between them. She licked her lips unthinkingly, and his gaze followed the movement, and he felt to the need to draw a deeper breath. The sexual tension between them was thick enough that he could have sliced it with a blade. She kept pace with him as he kept walking until he paused at a pair of tall gilded doors.

"Here is the library. Please follow me." He moved ahead of her and opened the door. Her little gasp made him smile. If there was one place that would garner such a reaction, it would be the library of Stormclyffe Hall.

"I've never…it's so…" Words seemed to fail her.

He laughed, genuinely pleased at her reaction. He had struck the little American speechless at least for the moment.

"This way, I'll take you to the family archives." Once more he had his hand on her lower back and guided her towards the documents, which would distract her for the rest of the day.

He hoped.

CHAPTER 3

A KISS. A TANGLE OF LIMBS, melding mouths, and a climax that had ripped her apart inside. It had changed her from the inside out. Jane rested her fingertips on her lips, falling deep into the hazy memory of their fiery passion.

It hadn't been a daydream. One minute they'd been talking and the next... Something had taken her over, and like a stranger in her own body, she'd flung herself at Bastian and kissed him—more than kissed him. He'd had his hand between her legs, and he had made her come. It was wild, insane, and erotic. It was also disturbing. If she hadn't known better, she might have thought she'd been possessed. When they were together, there was this electric charge that seemed to twine about them, tugging them closer and closer until they shared the same breath, the same heartbeat. Kissing Bastian had been natural and right, even though she'd never met him before in her life.

She had tried to act like what happened meant nothing, that some temporary passion had swept them both away, but she couldn't shake that feeling of sharing her body and losing control to someone else. And even more frighteningly, she couldn't erase the memory of her lips forming one name over and over as she came apart in his arms.

Richard.

Had the stories of this place gotten to her? Was she going mad from the stress of her dissertation and the desire to end the bizarre and nightmarish dreams that haunted her almost nightly? Those seemed like more plausible explanations, but she couldn't dismiss the sense that the answers to what was happening here and to her were just within reach. As though veiled by a cloud of mist, she couldn't make out the shapes clearly. Solutions and answers were buried deep in the mire and fog.

As she trailed behind Bastian, she was torn between admiring his tight ass molded in charcoal slacks and admiring the beautiful interior of the castle. He hadn't prepared her for the library though. Nothing could have.

None of the photographs of the Hall had ever revealed the library's interior. She had assumed it was because it was like any other library in any other castle or manor house. How wrong she was.

The room was awash in bold reds and a range of pale yellows to deep golds. Wall panels were decorated with art that looked so familiar.

"Is this what I think it is?" She pointed to one of the panels with a red-painted background and a Chinese scene in yellow.

His lips twitched. "If you're thinking of William Alexander's book *Views of China*, then you are correct. Richard apparently enjoyed the text immensely and had an artist replicate many of the etchings."

She smiled. "I can see why. The culture and the life…can you imagine what it must have been like for Alexander?" William Alexander had been an English watercolorist who visited China and made drawings of the scenery and life during his time there. His *Views of China* was a highly valued and much-admired work. Even the Brighton Pavilion Palace, which was built in Brighton for George, Prince of Wales as a seaside palace, boasted similar scenes inspired by Alexander's book.

Bastian's expression softened. "I would give so much to see through the eyes of the dead, to see what they have seen, to experience times I cannot fathom." He looked away then, his gaze roving the two-story-high shelves of the library, but Jane couldn't tear her attention from him.

How many women had fallen under his spell? A man haunted

by his family's past, a dedicated scholar, and as brooding and captivating as Lord Byron. If she let her thoughts run away with her, she knew Bastian would distract her from her dissertation.

Focus, Jane, focus.

The last thing she needed was to fall for him. After Tim, her heart couldn't take it. She'd only just managed to stitch the bleeding, torn organ back together. Bastian would not be the one to tear it apart again.

They strolled further into the room, and she tilted her head back to better admire the lotus-shaped chandeliers. Intricate paintings decorated each of the petals on every chandelier. In the middle of the wall to the right, a vast fireplace rose up with columns on either side, adorned with twining serpents. Unable to resist the urge, she hastened over to touch the pale Swedish green marble that formed the snake. The serpent's features had been sculpted so precisely that she half-expected it to come to life and bite her.

A massive mirror hung above the fireplace, and it reflected the windows on the opposite side of the library. A lush landscaped garden seemed to stretch for miles beyond the fireplace. The deceptive placing of the mirror created an enchanting illusion that one could walk through the mirror into an alternate world. A marble dragon perched atop the mirror's gilt-edged frame. Its wings were spread wide, jaws gaping open as it silently roared.

She gasped. A sudden flash of something wild and fearful ripped through her an instant before it was gone.

"Jane?" Bastian placed a hand on her shoulder, but then almost immediately he removed it and stepped back from her. "Are you well? You gave a little start just now."

She hastily nodded. "Yes, I'm fine. It's just…that dragon. It's so…" How could she describe having such a visceral reaction to a stone creature?

"Fierce. The beast is fierce." He crossed his arms over his chest, scowling back at the dragon.

She realized then she was still touching the serpent's head and pulled her hand away.

"Fierce indeed. I didn't expect such decorations in a library."

He chuckled. "The music room in the Pavilion in Brighton was modeled after Stormclyffe."

Ahh, I had guessed right then.

"My ancestor, Richard, believed something more…medieval would suit Stormclyffe. Our coat of arms bears a dragon after all. He designed the dragon to appear as you see them. The Pavilion's dragons are more complacent- looking and merely hold the curtains in place."

The eyes of the dragon seemed to watch her as she shifted from one foot to the other. It's long, angular snout looked ready to spew fire and puff smoke from its nostrils. The way it hunched over the mirror gave her the distinct impression it wasn't merely guarding the library, but rather hunting the library's inhabitants. It was an unsettling thought.

"You don't like it?" The earl teased her.

She nibbled her lip thoughtfully. "It's not that I don't like it. I just feel like it's watching me."

He grinned. "Don't tell me you are afraid? Isn't your dissertation connected to mysteries and hauntings? That's what your letters stated. I didn't think you would be so foolish as to pick a topic that would frighten you."

Before she even had time to think, she'd socked him in the shoulder again. She'd punched an earl. This was a bad habit she was forming.

He merely caught her by the shoulders, stilling her when she would have retreated from him. Their faces were so close that she could see endless books reflected in his gaze. He moved one hand up to cup her chin.

"Perhaps," he murmured huskily, "you should have directed your dissertation to something less threatening."

Brimming with anger, she bit back a viper-like retort and smiled sweetly. "Such as?"

The wicked glint in his eyes warned her he was going to say something infuriating.

"Why not write about the effects of wildflowers in various English counties? Surely that would inspire no fears?"

"Wildflowers?" She knocked his hand away from her chin and turned her back on him. *Provoking man.* She didn't have much of a natural temper, but what little was there, he found and prodded repeatedly until she broke and snapped at him. Still, she probably should be thankful. She and Tim had never fought; he'd never irritated her. She couldn't fall for someone when they drove her crazy. Bastian's ability to annoy her was therefore a small blessing.

"Oh come now, Jane," he said her name so softly, almost a croon, the way a man would to soften his lover's injured pride. That only made her more upset. He thought he could work some seductive magic to sidetrack her in her quest for research. The man was a nuisance. Couldn't he just leave her to the books and get on with his day? Instead he insisted on dragging her around the castle and teasing her.

She didn't reply. Not yet. When he came up behind her and gently placed a hand on her shoulder, turning her body back to face his, she finally had to meet his stare.

"What's the matter?" he asked.

"What's the matter? I could ask you the same question. You're teasing me and yet you—" She didn't dare finish. It felt like he was flirting with her, but maybe she was wrong. The last thing she wanted for him to think was that she viewed herself worthy of his attentions or that she wanted them. It would only complicate things. While she didn't mind, as she'd insisted to him earlier, that had been under the pretense of being allowed to stay and conduct her research. She hadn't actually thought she'd start to succumb to his charms. It was a good thing he had the ability to infuriate her as well. That made him far less attractive.

"Can you please just take me to the records?"

"Of course." His tone was more reserved. The wall that had started to crumble between them was solid again. "This way."

He led her to a shelf near the floor on the other side of the fireplace where several tall tomes were behind a sheet of glass. He bent, pressed his fingertips to the panel, and slid the glass to the side, making the large books accessible.

"Here are the recorded histories and family trees of the Weymouth line. I won't allow you access to any private letters or other documents from my family. I assume three-hundred years worth of information is enough to keep you occupied for the afternoon? I can guide to you other sources tomorrow." He paused, then leaned one shoulder against the bookshelves.

The man was hot when he leaned that way. Why did *leaning* have to be so damned sexy? Maybe it had to do with the way it called attention to the long, lithe shape of his legs and the muscles of his shoulders. She wanted to smack herself for even going there. She shouldn't be thinking about him like that. *Dissertation. Focus on your research.*

"That reminds me. Where are you staying? The trip to the town can be treacherous after dark. I wouldn't want you driving off the cliffs into the sea. I would prefer to have someone escort you back." He announced this casually but there was something odd in his expression, an emotion she couldn't read clearly.

Was he worried about her? She mentally shrugged it off. Of course he didn't care about her, not that way. After what had happened between them in the drawing room, she was hesitant to do anything that might give the wrong impression about her. He might not think of her at all in the way she was currently thinking about him. *Naked.* And how she'd like to get him out of those dark slacks and light gray sweater that molded to his broad chest muscles.

Bad idea. Must not think of him naked. She chastised herself. His offer probably stemmed from worries over a lawsuit from her family if she drove her rental car off the cliff and died.

"I've got a room booked at a little inn."

Bastian waved a hand. "Don't worry about that. Do your research this afternoon. I will drive you into town tonight around sunset."

"You'll drive me?" Weren't earls supposed to have chauffeurs?

"I do know how to drive." He flashed a mocking smile. "Even my ancestors drove their own sporting carriages. But to answer your question, my driver is still in London along with some of the other staff and won't move in until the restorations are complete.

I've actually been driving myself since I moved back here."

He sounded smug, as if he'd proved false her accusation that he couldn't operate a car. Had he taken her comment as an insult? God, she hoped not. She mentally kicked herself.

"Oh. Then yes, that would be fine."

"Excellent." He stepped away from the bookshelves. "I'll come to collect you later. Enjoy your research." He flashed her a cocky smile that did something funny to her knees before he took his leave and left her alone with the dragon and his hoard of jealously guarded books.

Jane removed the first of several volumes from the shelf and carried it to a nearby reading table. A cloud of dust billowed up as she set the book down on the polished cherry wood. The motes twirled and danced through the stray beams of light from the high windows. A heavy silence filled the library, almost tangible. Each movement Jane made elicited a loud sound: the whisk of paper as she removed it from her briefcase, the rapid click of her ballpoint pen as she pressed the cap with her thumb. She collected her materials and opened her notebook to a fresh page, hoping to dispel the eerie silence of the room by losing herself in the text on the pages before her.

She peeled back the heavy brown leather cover of the book. The first few pages were blank, but the third bore an elaborate sketch of a family tree. The names were inscribed with a quill pen, the ink faded to a pale brown but still legible. She carefully took notes and replicated the tree, which started with births and marriages in 1607.

For the next three hours, she remained in her chair, diligently recording the Weymouth earldom's history from the births to the deaths of its more prominent family members. Until Richard's death, the Weymouth line seemed normal in its deaths and births. After Richard's passing, the pattern changed showing an extraordinary amount of tragic deaths and accidents. There were people drowning at sea, falling from ladders in the orchards, and unexpected infant deaths. A majority of the victims were women who had married into the Stormclyffe family. There were many more gruesome deaths and more unexplained accidents or occurrences. Fires broke out in the castle several times, always starting in bedrooms where the women who married into the Weymouth family were sleeping. Crops on the estate failed for several years while the crops of the farmers from the surrounding areas thrived.

Cursed. Maybe the rumors were right. The entire family seemed truly cursed.

She set her pen down and closed the large tome. It didn't seem to matter whether it was supernatural or merely bad lack—the facts didn't lie. Since Richard's bride jumped to her death in 1811, the family line and home had suffered through a nearly endless chronology of heartbreak.

The last entry in the record book stated a fact she hadn't known.

Bastian's father had died in a car accident at the age of forty-three. When she had investigated Bastian's background, she hadn't focused on his parents. She knew logically that since he was the current Earl of Weymouth, it meant his father must have passed away, but there were no records detailing how. Only Bastian and his mother survived. If Bastian stuck true to his words that he would never marry, that meant he wouldn't continue his family's line. The title would pass to distant cousins, but the direct line would perish.

She'd judged him too harshly, thinking him a fool for not wanting to marry. Now she wondered if he wouldn't commit to building a future with anyone because so many tragic and untimely deaths weighed the family tree down. Even if he refused to believe in the curse, perhaps somewhere deep in the recesses of his mind lay a fear of bringing another child into this world under the Weymouth title. Tears burned at the corners of her eyes. How devastating to believe, even subconsciously, that any baby he might have could be condemned to death by his family's curse. It would explain why he kept himself emotionally distant from others. His playboy reputation might make her blush, but the man himself was a still a mystery.

A muscle cramped in her neck. A series of small knots had formed after hours of her head bending over the desk. She pushed her research materials across the table and reached behind her to massage the area, soothing the tension away.

As far as her dissertation was concerned, she could use the chronology of deaths and disasters of the family to highlight their influence on myths and legends around this particular estate. She would work it into the stories connected to other estates around England. If she was able to talk Bastian into letting her photograph or perhaps scan the copies of the family tree with particular entries regarding some of the deaths of the family members, she would be able to cite them as primary sources.

The sun emerged from the clouds, causing long shadows to stretch along the carpeted floor. She watched their slow-moving progress for several minutes as the darkness consumed the patterned carpet. One shadow seemed to move more quickly than the others. It expanded rapidly, consuming the light on the table closest to the window. An identifiable shape began to form.

A dragon.

Her gaze shot up to the windows, and she expected to see a bird spreading its wings in a nearby tree, which would have explained the unusual shape. But there were no trees visible through the glass. The dragon shadow twisted its head, and its tail lashed out in a whip-like flash. Its wings spread wide, and for a brief second, she thought she could hear a distant roar and feel the library's floor quake beneath her.

She cried out and leapt from her chair, backing up until she hit the bookcase behind her. Something crashed to the floor at her feet, but she dared not look. Her heart pounded against her ribs as she searched for the shadow, which seemed to have vanished as quickly as it had appeared.

As her breathing slowed, and the faint ringing in her ears faded, she glanced down and noticed the small leather-bound book on the floor. It was partially open over one of her feet. Bending down, she gingerly picked it up and studied it more closely. The pages were full, but not with printed text. Instead, each page was filled with scrawling handwriting, the archaic cursive style beautiful and half-faded. Dates were inscribed in the top left corner.

It was a diary.

Transfixed, she sank back into her seat and began to read. As she read, she could see it all unfold as though she were a visitor there, watching unseen like a ghost.

> *April 21ˢᵗ, 1810*
>
> *I was pouring over the Hall's account books my steward had prepared for me. The task was wearisome but necessary. I longed to have a distraction, something that could take my mind off of my concerns. Sir Lionel Huntington had written to say he would be visiting again this afternoon to discuss the future of his daughter, Cordelia. While I am ready to take a bride, I'm not sure she is the one for me. Sir Lionel was apparently determined to see his daughter become the Countess of Weymouth. The chit is pretty enough. Honey blond hair and hazel eyes. But there is a coldness to Miss Huntington's demeanor and presence that unnerves me. What's more, her family bears a rather dark history, one that I fear I cannot completely overlook. They are descendents of a woman who was accused of witchcraft in Lancashire. She was proven innocent, but I cannot help but wonder still… Does darkness run through the veins of her female lineage? Sometimes I see Miss Huntington's eyes gleam in a way that makes me wonder and worry.*

A light rap on my study door disturbed my thoughts.

"Enter," I called out.

My butler, Mr. Shrewsbury, poked his gray-haired head around the edge of the door.

"The new innkeeper, Mr. Braxton, is here to see you my lord. I have put him and his daughter in the red drawing room."

"Thank you, Shrewsbury." Relief poured through me.

Finally, an excuse to escape the accounts. I am interested in meeting Mr. Braxton. Since he is a new resident to the town, it is important that I meet with the man and establish good relations with him.

I pushed back my chair and stood, checking my appearance. My trousers were clean, my waistcoat unwrinkled, a veritable miracle given that I'd spent the last few hours slumped over my desk during my labors. With a hasty hand run through my hair, I was satisfied I looked suitable for company and headed towards the drawing room.

It is my favorite room, one full of light and color. It boasts of a fair amount of books and paintings of my family from years before. A pair of loveseats face each other with a small table next to each where a tea tray could be placed for visitors. When I entered, I found Mr. Braxton perched on one of the two love seats. A maid set a tray of tea and biscuits on the table next to him.

"My lord!" Braxton got to his feet immediately, a genuine smile on his face. With ruddy cheeks and a muscled figure barely concealed by his tailored waistcoat, Braxton was a fit and amiable man.

"Welcome to my home, Mr. Braxton. I am delighted you were able to come and meet with me." I immediately sought out the man's daughter, expecting a plump, whey-faced creature. The woman stood in the far corner with her back to me as she admired my books.

My first thought was how lovely her figure was. When she turned to face me, my heart stopped. The world came to an abrupt halt. I couldn't breathe. She was so beautiful, something deep in my chest began to hurt. There was a fire in her eyes and warmth in her smile. The blush in her cheeks was becoming, and the dark curls that framed her face accented her creamy skin. I was lost to her in that moment. I wondered if I would never want another woman except her.

"My lord," Miss Braxton's voice was husky and a little breathless, as though she was reacting to me much in the same way I reacted to her. I hoped so. I did not wish to be the only one so completely affected.

"Miss Braxton, it is a pleasure." I strode up to her and bent over the hand she offered hesitantly. I pressed a kiss to her skin. The scent of rosewater filled my nose. The delicate perfume was a perfect accent to the woman who wore it.

"Thank you for extending an offer to visit." Mr. Braxton appeared at his daughter's side, reminding me that I and Miss Braxton were not alone, no matter how much I might wish we were.

"Of course. Please sit." I gestured to the settees, and we all took our seats.

I spent the next hour conversing with Braxton about Weymouth and how best to settle in with the local folk. Unlike many of the other inns in the county, Braxton's accommodations were of a higher quality, and many aristocrats would likely wish to stay at the new inn as they passed through on their way to the other parts of England. Despite the conversation distracting me, I managed to keep my eyes on Miss Braxton. I relished the way she kept glancing at my books with keen interest. I suspected she must be a lady who enjoyed reading and wasn't merely a fair-faced creature with no real thoughts in her head. Women with no interests and no intellectual pursuits held no appeal for me.

As the conversation came to its natural end, I bid my guests good-bye with the invitation for them to return on the morrow for dinner. As I watched Miss Braxton and her father depart, a piece of my soul seemed to separate from my body and accompany her home. I had never felt such a kindred spirit in anyone, man or woman. Come the morrow, I knew I would be desperate for a glimpse of her. Dinner could not come soon enough.

ABOUT THE AUTHOR

LAUREN SMITH IS AN ATTORNEY by day, author by night, who pens adventurous and edgy romance stories by the light of her smart phone flashlight app. She's a native Oklahoman who lives with her three pets—a feisty chinchilla, sophisticated cat and dapper little schnauzer. She's won multiple awards in several romance subgenres including being an Amazon.com Breakthrough Novel Award Quarter-Finalist and a Semi-Finalist for the Mary Wollstonecraft Shelley Award.

Check her out at **www.laurensmithbooks.com**

You can follow her on Facebook at
www.facebook.com/LaurenDianaSmith

On Twitter at **@LSmithAuthor**

Her blog is **www.theleagueofrogues.blogspot.com**

www.ingramcontent.com/pod-product-compliance
Lightning Source LLC
Chambersburg PA
CBHW021020120726
47905CB00009B/3109